**Praise for Kate Hoffmann
from *RT Book Reviews***

The Charmer

"Hoffmann's deeply felt, emotional story is riveting.
It's impossible to put down."

Your Bed or Mine?

"Fully developed characters and perfect pacing
make this story feel completely right."

Doing Ireland!

"Sexy and wildly romantic."

The Mighty Quinns: Ian

"A very hot story mixes with great characters to
make every page a delight."

Who Needs Mistletoe?

"Romantic, sexy and heartwarming."

The Mighty Quinns: Teague

"Sexy, heartwarming and romantic...a story to
settle down with and enjoy—and then re-read."

Blaze

Dear Reader,

The Traveling Quinn Saga continues this month, with Cameron Quinn hopping on a bus that will take him to Vulture Creek, New Mexico. What kind of new life will he find there, do you suppose? His two brothers, Dermot and Kieran, have already found love in Wisconsin and Kentucky. And next month, Ronan, the youngest Quinn, will end up in over his head in Maine.

This series has been a lot of fun to write, especially since I've been able to explore four different settings. Choosing the place my characters come to life is one of my favorite parts of writing. Researching a new location and then weaving the details into my hero and heroine's journey is always a challenge, but it's one I love to take on.

After writing almost seventy books, I really should go back and see how many states I've visited in my stories. Too bad I can't deduct literary mileage on my tax returns!

All the best,

Kate Hoffmann

Kate Hoffmann

THE MIGHTY QUINNS: CAMERON

HARLEQUIN®
entertain, enrich, inspire™

Recycling programs
for this product may
not exist in your area.

ISBN-13: 978-0-373-79716-5

THE MIGHTY QUINNS: CAMERON

Copyright © 2012 by Peggy A. Hoffmann

www.Harlequin.com

Printed in U.S.A.

ABOUT THE AUTHOR

Kate Hoffmann has written more than 70 books for Harlequin, most of them for the Temptation and the Blaze lines. She spent time as a music teacher, a retail assistant buyer and an advertising exec before she settled into a career as a full-time writer. She continues to pursue her interests in music, theatre and musical theatre, working with local schools in various productions. She lives in southeastern Wisconsin with her cat, Chloe.

Books by Kate Hoffmann

Prologue

A DAMP WIND BUFFETED the mourners standing around the grave site. Cameron Quinn stared up into the slate-gray sky, then closed his eyes against the tears that threatened. He couldn't remember the last time the sun had shone. It had been a year of dark, gloomy days strung together with nights of strange and disturbing dreams.

Cameron held tight to the umbrella as it was buffeted by the wind. His younger twin brothers, Dermot and Kieran, stood on one side of him, huddling close more for comfort than for protection from the coming rain. Ronan, his youngest brother, stood in front of him, his posture stiff, his hands shoved in his coat pockets.

After a year of searching and waiting and wondering, it was finally over. Jamie and Suzanne Quinn had been declared dead. Cameron's parents had been due to arrive in Vanuatu in the South Pacific a little more than a year ago, ferrying a sailing yacht across the Pacific for a wealthy buyer.

The trip was originally meant to be a summer vacation for the whole family, but when the owner pushed up the delivery date, Cameron and his three brothers had been forced to stay behind for school. The trip was to take just over a month.

Cameron and the younger Quinns had marked off the calendar on their grandfather's kitchen wall as each day passed. Every few days, they'd heard from their parents via satellite phone, but then their parents missed a night and then another. A week passed and the boys could sense the worry in their grandfather's demeanor. And yet Suzanne and Jamie weren't officially missing. And then they were.

"Why are we burying a—a box?" Kieran asked.

"Coffin," Cameron murmured. "It's called a coffin."

Dermot drew a ragged breath. "What if they come home? Will we dig it up again and get our stuff back?"

Cameron glanced down at his brother and shook his head. "They're not going to come home." Though he wanted to believe differently, Cameron knew the reality of their situation.

A week after the planned arrival date, the search for his parents had begun. Two weeks later, there was still no word, no sign, no explanation. And after his parents were a month overdue, a harsh truth began to creep into the boys' lives. Their parents might be lost. Perhaps they were adrift in a life raft, or captured by pirates, or marooned on some tropical island. No one could say for sure, not even Cameron's grandfather. And he always had answers for the questions his four grandsons asked.

It was not knowing the truth that bothered Cameron the most. That tiny flicker of hope that refused to fade. For a year, he'd believed, along with his brothers, that this would all turn out to be a very bad dream. But as he watched the empty casket being lowered into the dark hole in the earth, that flicker of hope faded, then extinguished.

"I'm scared," Ronan said, turning to face Cameron, his eyes swimming with tears.

Cameron wrapped his free arm around Ronan's shoulders. "Don't be scared. We're going to be all right. I promise."

Dermot brushed a tear from his cheek. "I want Ma and Da back. I know they're coming back. I know it."

"Me, too," Kieran said. "They're coming back."

"Maybe," Cameron said. He wanted more than anything to believe. Maybe he shouldn't give up quite yet. There was always a chance, wasn't there? For now, he'd let his little brothers believe. They'd come to their own realizations in time.

The memories of their parents would fade, life would go on, and they'd accept the truth. Nothing would ever be easy or simple or silly again. It was Cameron's job to hold the family together, to be mother and father to his younger brothers. He wasn't sure he was up to the job, but he'd do his best. He owed his parents that much.

1

THE BUS STOPPED in front of a worn-down café, a neon beer sign in the window flickering with the only color Cameron Quinn had seen in the past two hundred miles. "Home-cooked meals," he murmured as he stared at the sign. At least Vulture Creek, New Mexico, had one thing going for it. From what he'd seen so far, the place was a dusty crossroad, somewhere on the way to Albuquerque.

He grabbed his leather duffel from the rack above his head and walked to the front of the bus, the aisle clear. None of the other passengers had chosen this destination, and after seeing the town out the window, he figured they could count themselves lucky. They were obviously on their way to more glamorous locations, like Santa Fe and Amarillo and Tulsa. A few passengers were even headed to Roswell to take in the "alien" experience.

Cameron knew exactly how those aliens felt, dropping down into a barren, almost lifeless world.

He'd come from Seattle, where it rained almost every day of the year and where green, not brown, was the predominant color. He stepped off the bus and squinted up at the turquoise sky, shading his eyes with his hand. It was the only sight that assured him he was still on planet Earth.

Moments later, the bus pulled away in a cloud of dust and diesel fumes. This would be home for the next six weeks, this desolate spot that looked more like the surface of the moon than a habitable location.

Why had his grandfather picked Vulture Creek? The name alone was enough to scare away most people. The challenge had been simple—in theory. His grandfather had sent his four grandsons to strange corners of the country on a quest of sorts—a quest to find out who they really were and where they belonged. Dermot was somewhere in Wisconsin, Kieran in Tennessee, Ronan in Maine, and Cameron, the eldest of the four, was banished to the middle of nowhere.

For six weeks, they were supposed carve out an existence for themselves, away from the family business and familiar surroundings. In theory, he understood his grandfather's motives. He and his brothers had worked for the family business, Quinn Yachtworks, since shortly after their parents went missing, pitching in to do anything to make the business succeed. There hadn't really been a choice in the matter; they'd just done it to repay their grandfather for taking them in and to stave off the grief that hung over the family like a dark cloud.

But now it was time to decide the fate of the successful company they'd helped build. An attractive offer to buy the business had come along from an interested party, and Martin Quinn had a decision to make—leave the business to his grandsons or sell and retire in luxury.

Cameron had never really thought twice about what he did for a living. He'd felt obligated to work at the family business, and he enjoyed his position as head of the design team. It suited his artistic inclinations and paid well—and it was interesting work.

It also suited his personality. He liked the solitary pursuit of the perfect design. He was in control; he made the decisions. It was a quiet life, a controlled life and one that he'd grown quite accustomed to. There were never any surprises.

So it wasn't any wonder he thought this "vacation" was an exercise in futility. Cameron knew exactly where he belonged and what he was meant to do. He knew it from the moment he became head of his family, from the day his parents had officially been proclaimed dead. It had been his responsibility to watch over his younger brothers, to make their life with their grandfather work.

Sure, he'd had other dreams. When he was a kid, he'd wanted to become a paleontologist, like the hero in *Jurassic Park*. He'd fantasized about exotic locations and complicated digs, of discoveries that would turn history upside down. But he put those dreams aside for the greater good of his family.

According to their grandfather's plan, after six weeks, he and his brothers were to return home. If they wanted to make a commitment to the company, they could. If they wanted to carve out a new life somewhere else, then all would be well. If they all chose a different life, then they'd share in the profits from the sale and build something new for themselves.

He crossed the street to the diner. He'd have a decent meal, check out the town and then buy a bus ticket for the nearest civilized city. After all, Vulture Creek was neither a hotbed of employment opportunities nor a glamorous vacation destination. Surely his grandfather didn't expect him to live here for six weeks. He'd bide his time someplace more comfortable.

As he opened the door of the diner, a pickup truck slowly passed by. From beneath the brim of a battered cowboy hat, the driver watched Cameron with a suspicious glare. Cameron gave him a nod, but the man didn't acknowledge the greeting. "Hospitable place," he muttered to himself.

A bell above the door rang as Cameron entered the café. Fans hung from the high ceilings, turning slowly yet doing nothing to freshen the air. A small crowd of people was gathered around tables near the window, the remains of their breakfast still scattered in front of them. They were laughing and arguing, but Cameron ignored them and sat down at the empty counter. He glanced to the back of the diner and saw a woman sitting in a booth near the door to the kitchen, talking on her cell phone.

He relaxed on the stool and grabbed a menu, studying the prices. He had about six dollars left in cash and a pocketful of change. But his grandfather had given them all a company credit card to use, as well. He'd pull that out for lunch and then find a cheap motel room with a hot shower and a soft bed.

A middle-aged woman stepped through the swinging door, a coffeepot in her hand. She strolled up to him and set a cup in front of him. Her blue blouse was embroidered with her name—Millie. "Coffee?"

Cameron shook his head. It was too hot to drink coffee. "Ice water," he said. "The biggest glass you have."

"Breakfast specials are Denver omelet, blueberry waffles, and steak and eggs," she said, observing him with a keen eye. "Lunch specials are pork enchiladas and a meat-loaf plate. We also have chicken-dumpling soup and grasshopper pie made fresh this morning. What can I get you?"

Cameron glanced at the clock above the counter. Though it was only eleven, he really didn't feel much like breakfast. "I'll have the meat loaf," Cameron said. "With fries. And the soup. Do you have beer on tap?"

"Just bottles."

"Give me a bottle of your best. And you take credit cards?"

"MasterCard and Visa," she said.

She returned with his beer and poured it into a glass mug that looked like a cowboy boot. Cameron took a long, slow sip of it. He glanced over at the booth and silently observed the woman he'd noticed earlier. His breath caught in his throat as she turned slightly, and he coughed, the beer going down his windpipe.

Her battered straw cowboy hat had hidden her features, but she'd tipped her chin up to reveal a stunning profile. He found himself staring at her mouth as she spoke. She was younger than he'd originally thought, in her mid-twenties. And there was something different about her, something slightly exotic. His mind drifted as he thought about that mouth, the lush lips, wondering if the rest of her body was as tantalizingly sexy.

When she hung up the phone, he turned his attention back to his beer, watching her in the reflection of the mirror behind the counter. He held his breath, waiting for her to move. But when he noticed a distinct limp in her gait, he glanced back down at his beer, uneasy with his reaction to her handicap.

Though he felt sorry for her, nothing as insignificant as a limp could erase the image of perfection he found when he considered her beautiful features and her slender body. To his surprise, she sat down a few seats away and dropped her cowboy hat on the counter.

"Millie, I'm gonna grab myself a coffee," she called toward the kitchen door, tucking a strand of raven hair behind her ear. She circled around the end of the counter and picked up a cup, then filled it from the pot.

God, she was beautiful, Cameron mused. This was the last place on earth he expected to find an interesting woman, and this one elicited more curiosity in him than any woman he'd seen in the past five years. She was clad in faded jeans and a baggy chambray shirt, not the typical fashions for the women he usually lusted after. Dusty cowboy boots completed the look.

She took a sip of her coffee, staring straight ahead. Cameron grabbed the opportunity to take in the details of her face. High cheekbones and dark eyes betrayed a Native American heritage, but there was something else there, something that softened her stunning features just a bit.

"Is it considered polite to stare at people where you come from?" she asked, her gaze still fixed on the coffeepot. She slowly turned and gave him a cool look, her raven eyebrow raised quizzically.

"Sorry," Cameron murmured. "I've just been stuck on a bus for the past few days with nothing interesting to look at." He chuckled softly. "And you're the absolute last thing I thought I'd see in this place."

"And what exactly am I?"

"Interesting," he murmured. Cameron took another sip of his beer. "Sorry. I'll keep my eyes to myself."

She turned away, as if embarrassed by the compliment. "You have been on a bus too long," she said.

"I have."

A long silence grew between them as they both stared straight ahead, enjoying their drinks.

"What are you doing in Vulture Creek?" she asked.

"It's a long story."

"Where are you from?"

"Seattle," he said. "Washington."

"I know where Seattle is," she said with a smile.

"Of course you do," he said. For someone who didn't want to be noticed, she sure was trying awfully hard to strike up a conversation. Cameron had never been an expert at small talk, but just this once, it might be nice to make an effort. "Do you live around here?"

She seemed to be understandably suspicious of him. "Around," she replied.

"That's a little vague," he said. "Around here? Around New Mexico? Around the Southwest?"

"Albuquerque," she said.

"And what are you doing in Vulture Creek?" he asked.

She smiled. "It's a long story."

Cameron chuckled softly. "Well, that does it, then. I've found someone who is worse at small talk than

I am. Maybe we should just stop talking altogether before we bore each other to death."

She shrugged. "Fine by me. You're the one who started the conversation."

"Actually, you were the first one to speak, as I recall. I was just staring."

"Well, I'm done speaking. Starting now."

Millie appeared a few minutes later with Cameron's lunch. She set the plate in front of him, then nodded toward his empty mug. "Another beer?"

"Sure," Cameron said as he dug into his meal.

Millie turned to the woman sitting next to him. "What can I get for you, Sofie? Breakfast or lunch?"

"The meat loaf is good," Cameron said between bites. Sofie. Was that short for Sofia? The name suited her, he thought to himself. Sofia, the dark, exotic beauty with the lush mouth and the sparkling eyes.

"I'll have a grilled-cheese and a cup of soup," Sofie said.

"Can I get you anything else?" Millie asked Cameron.

"A job. Do you know of anyone who's looking to hire? I need work. And a place to stay."

She nodded toward the group sitting at the tables near the front of the diner. "You could talk to the professor over there," she said. "He has a dinosaur dig out in the desert. They're always looking for help."

Cameron gasped. "Really. A dig?" He shook his head in disbelief. Was this why his grandfather had sent him to Vulture Creek? Did he know about the dig?

"They don't pay," Sofie said. "Other than meals. They're looking for volunteers."

"Aren't you looking for someone, Sofie?" Millie asked.

"No," Sofie said.

"Sure you are. You mentioned it yesterday. I distinctly remember you saying you didn't have enough eyes or ears to cover all the ground you needed to. I do believe those were your words."

"What kind of work do you do?" Cameron asked.

"She's a private investigator," Millie said. "Working on a big case." The waitress wandered back to the kitchen, leaving Sofie and Cameron with another uncomfortable silence.

Cameron sighed softly. Though the dinosaur dig was intriguing, he'd have to find a way to make some real money. And if Sofie, the private investigator, had a job, then he ought to explore that option. Who knew if there would even be other opportunities in Vulture Creek?

"So do you or don't you have a job you're looking to fill?"

Millie set a cup of soup in front of Sofie. "Maybe you ought to interview him. He looks like a clever young man." She winked at Cameron. "Careful, now. If you have any secrets, she'll find a way to get them out of you."

Cameron stifled a smile. Actually, that sounded

like a lot of fun. Though he wasn't much of a conversationalist, he was enjoying the back-and-forth with Sofie. Beneath that cool, composed exterior, Cameron suspected there was a fiery, passionate woman. He was curious to catch a glimpse of that side of her.

"Why are you here?" Sofie asked.

Cameron wiped his hands with his napkin and swallowed the mouthful of meat loaf. "I'm here because my grandfather sent me here. I'm supposed to take the next six weeks to figure out what I want to do with the rest of my life."

"Why would you need to do that?"

"My grandfather owns the family business. I work there. He needs to make some decisions about the future of that business. He wants us all to be sure of where we want to be."

"All?"

"Me and my three brothers. We all work for the company."

"What do you do? I mean, for a job?" she replied.

"I design sailing yachts," he said.

Sofie laughed and nodded to Millie. "Well, we have a lot of sailing yachts here in the desert," she said. "I really don't think I have—"

"Sofie," Cameron said.

She stopped talking and watched him warily. "Yes?"

"I'm a smart guy. I'm pretty sure I can handle whatever you send my way. Why don't you give me a chance? If it doesn't work out, you can fire me."

"What's your name?" she finally asked.

He held out his hand. "Cameron Quinn. Most people call me Cam."

Reluctantly, she shook his hand. "Sofia Reyes," she said softly. "Most people call me Sofie."

The moment he touched her, the sensation of her skin against his sent a flood of warmth racing through his veins. He didn't want to let her hand go, but forced himself. "Now that we've met, you have to let me buy you lunch," Cameron said. "You can tell me all about the virtues of Vulture Creek."

"That would be a very short lunch. More like a snack."

"Go ahead," Millie urged. "Let the man buy you lunch."

He felt a small measure of satisfaction when she nodded in agreement. Though he hadn't held out much hope of finding anything of interest in Vulture Creek when he stepped off the bus, his prospects were getting better with every minute that passed. Sofie Reyes. Even her name was sexy.

SOFIE SIGHED SOFTLY as she took her first bite of Millie's banana-cream pie. She'd been hanging around Vulture Creek for the past few weeks, and a slice of Millie's homemade pie had become a daily ritual for her.

"I think pie is just about the perfect food," Sofie said, emphasizing her statement with her fork. "You can eat it for breakfast, lunch or dinner. And it's good for a snack, too."

"I think you might be right," Cameron replied, digging into the apple pie he'd ordered after his own meal.

The conversation was easy between them, which Sofie found odd. She usually wasn't very comfortable around charming men, especially men she didn't know. Her instincts usually tended to have her second-guessing everything that was said, looking for ulterior motives and hidden meanings. It was the side effects of working as a private investigator, she knew. Everyone she met was guilty of something.

But this man, this Cameron Quinn, should have set off all her alarms. His reasons for being in Vulture Creek were cloudy at best. His wardrobe was more suited to a man who drove an expensive European sports car than a guy who took the Greyhound. And yet she couldn't help but be attracted.

In truth, she did need help. It had become almost impossible to cover all her bases with the case she was working, especially when she had to provide round-the-clock surveillance. And as a woman, she was more conspicuous in a small town like Vulture Creek. For whatever reason, people noticed her and they remembered her.

The sooner she wrapped up this case, the better, and if Cameron Quinn could help, who was she to refuse? She'd been chasing cheating husbands and deadbeat dads for almost six months, and it was wearing on her nerves. As soon as she was physically able, she'd be back on the job with the Albuquerque Police Department, back doing the job she was meant to do.

Sofie drew a deep breath. It had been two years since the accident, two years of recovery that seemed to progress an inch at a time. As much as she didn't want to face it, she knew the reality of her situation.

She might not make it back. She might never be able to pass the physical again. All she'd be left with was a hip that ached in the cold and a limp that made her the object of either pity or curiosity. Though she might be considered attractive, she was still damaged.

Most men never saw beyond the imperfection. Hell, she couldn't get beyond it herself most days. But sitting here, talking to Cameron, she could almost forget the flaw. He had a way of looking at her that made her feel as if she was the most fascinating woman he'd ever set eyes upon. And Sofie hadn't felt that way in a very long time. Not since the "incident."

Sofie came from a family of law-enforcement officers. Her father was a cop in Albuquerque, and each of her five brothers worked in criminal justice. So it was only natural that Sofie, the youngest in the family, had set her sights on the same career.

She'd begun work with the Albuquerque P.D. the year she graduated from college, and it had been a dream job. She'd worked her way up through the ranks and was undercover in Narcotics by the time she was twenty-six. Her team was in the midst of a major trafficking case when she got caught in a turf war between two rival drug gangs.

Sofie had known the dangers, but they'd been so close to making their case. She hadn't listened to her instincts or her superiors, believing that she could handle whatever came her way. But a speeding car and a half-crazed driver put her safety in someone else's hands. And the resulting crash had put her in intensive care for three months.

"You want another piece of pie?"

Sofie blinked, then glanced up from her empty plate. "What?"

"Pie," Cam said. "The way you were looking, I was thinking you might just eat the plate." He turned and searched for Millie. "Can we get another slice of the banana-cream pie?"

"No," she said, shaking her head. "I'm fine."

"I'm not," he said. "I'll have a piece of that banana-cream pie, please."

He sent her a smile, and Sofie felt a shiver skitter through her. Was she just imagining it, or was there an attraction between them? Sofie felt it, but was it mutual, or was it merely wishful thinking on her part?

Just because they'd indulged in a little casual flirting over lunch didn't mean that he was ready to pull her into his arms and ravish her. Cameron seemed like the kind of guy who kept a pretty tight leash on his desires.

Besides, if she decided against hiring him, he'd probably be on a bus out of Vulture Creek before she could find something else to like about him, rolling down the road like a tumbleweed in a dust storm.

Millie wandered over with the coffeepot and another slice of pie. She filled their cups, then slipped the check onto the counter beside Cameron. He pulled out his wallet and handed her a credit card, then turned back to Sofie. She reached into her back pocket for money, but Cameron brushed her hand aside. "It's on me," he said.

"That's not necessary. I can—"

"No, I want to." He paused. "I was thinking maybe you might be able to help me find a place to stay here in town. Maybe show me around?"

She wanted to say yes, to imagine that this day might go on a little longer. But she did have work to do. "Sure," she said. "I have some time." Work could wait a few hours.

As he finished up his dessert, Millie returned, a scowl on her face. She handed Cameron his credit card. "It wouldn't go through," she said. "There was a flag on the account for me to call, and they said to take away the card."

"What?" Cameron grabbed the card and stared at it. "But it's my—" He cursed softly, then chuckled. "Oh. Okay, I get it."

Sofie quickly stood. "What's going on?"

"My grandfather is making sure that I stay in Vulture Creek," he said, waving the card. He pulled out his wallet and riffled through the bills. "I have six dollars left. How the hell can I—"

"You need a job, son," Millie said.

"Yeah. And the sooner the better. All right, first things first. I need to pay for lunch."

"I've got some dishes piled up," Millie said. "And those windows out front need washing. That should about cover it."

"I can do that," Cameron agreed. "I'll start with the dishes. And maybe, if you've got something else I can do, I can build up a credit."

Sofie stood, then reached into the back pocket of her jeans and pulled out the wad of cash. A guy willing to wash dishes in a diner to pay his bill couldn't be all bad, could he? She peeled off enough to cover the lunch and a tip for Millie. "That should take care of it," she said. "You can pay me back later," she said to Cameron. "Come on."

Turning on her heel, she headed to the door. Everything inside her told her that this guy wasn't what he said he was. But at the same time, he seemed nice enough. She'd just maintain her distance until she was sure. She glanced over her shoulder to find him standing there. "You're hired."

He picked up his bag and ran after her, pushing the door open for her. "Thanks," he said. "Hey, you can take the lunch out of my first day's pay." He paused. "You are going to pay me, aren't you?"

"Yes."

"And I'm going to need a place to stay."

"We'll figure that out later," she said.

"I'd kind of like to get it figured out now," he said. "I've only got six dollars to my name."

"Sheriff Wendall lets people sleep in the jail when it's not occupied. But I think I can find you a place to bed down."

"Great," he said. He held out the six dollars and she waved him off.

"But before you start work for me, I have to do a background check," she said, putting her straw hat back on her head. She stood in front of him, her hands hitched on her waist, observing him shrewdly. "Is there anything in your past that you'd like to confess to right now? Because, I guarantee, by the end of the day, I'll know everything about you."

"A background check? What do you want to know?"

Sofie stared at him for a long moment. In truth, she wanted to know what it felt like to kiss him. She wanted to know whether he tasted half as good as he looked. She wanted to know what his naked body looked like beneath those fancy clothes and what it would take for her to get him out of his clothes and into her bed. And she—

"I don't have any secrets," he said.

She blinked, startled out of her daydream. Sofie cleared her throat. "How old are you? Where were you born? What do your parents do?"

"I'll be thirty in two months, I was born in Seattle, and my parents died when I was a kid. At least I think they're dead."

Sofie saw the look that crossed his face, a mix of resignation and pain. "I'm sorry. I didn't mean to bring up—"

"That's all right," he said, shrugging. "I don't mind talking about it."

"You said you thought they were dead. Don't you know for sure?" She sucked in a sharp breath. Though her first instinct was to interrogate, she realized that there was a polite limit to her questions. "Sorry. You don't have to answer that."

"They disappeared while ferrying a yacht across the Pacific. We don't know if they were lost in a storm and sank or drowned or what happened. One day they were there, and the next day, they'd disappeared. What about your folks? Are they alive?"

Sofie regretted questioning him in such a businesslike manner, but she wasn't about to drive out into the desert with a guy she couldn't trust. "My father is a cop. And my mother is an artist. They live in Albuquerque, where my mother has a gallery."

"And how old are you?"

"I'm asking the questions," she said.

"You're quite good at this," he said. "You're making me kind of nervous."

"I've had training. Do you have a photo ID with you?"

Cameron pulled out his wallet and handed her his Washington state driver's license. Sofie groaned inwardly. He even managed to look gorgeous on his license photo. This man was just too good to be true.

"Anything else you'd like to know?"

She shook her head. "I guess that will do for now." She gave him back his license.

"Good."

Sofie pointed to a battered Jeep sitting a short walk down the main street. When they reached it, Cameron tossed his bag in the backseat and hopped it. The Jeep had no doors, so he fastened his seat belt and braced his feet against the floor.

Sofie slid into the driver's side and grabbed a pair of sunglasses off the dash. "We're going to need to get you a proper hat," she said.

"Like yours?"

She grinned, then took her hat off and placed it on his head. "Yeah, just like mine," she said, turning the key in the ignition. "It's a good look on you."

Sofie made a wide U-turn and headed east out of town. Though her thoughts still strayed into fantasyland when she looked at the handsome stranger sitting beside her, at least she had a reason to keep him close by. She needed an extra set of eyes and ears to investigate the case she was working on. And with his looks and charm, he'd be the perfect undercover investigator.

2

"WHERE ARE WE GOING?" Cameron shouted.

"Into town," Sofie said over the sound of the wind and the Jeep.

"Weren't we just in town?"

She shook her head. "We're going to Holman. It's a bigger town. I'm going to check you out, and then, if you're cool, we're going to get you some work clothes and get started."

"So tell me about the case," he said.

"I'm working for a woman whose husband may or may not be cheating on her. There's a prenup, but she needs proof before she can file for divorce. Her family has a lot of money and he's a pretty powerful guy in Albuquerque politics. It's going to be a messy divorce."

"What do I do?"

"Mostly anything I can't," she said. "No one knows you, and as a guy, you can go places that I can't without being noticed."

"Like where?"

"Strip clubs," she said. "Roadhouses."

"You're going to make me go to a strip club?" Cameron asked. He chuckled to himself. Now, this was a job he could get behind.

Maybe his grandfather had the right idea. When would he ever have had the chance to be a private investigator? It was the last thing in the world he could imagine doing for a living. He sat back and turned his face up into the sun.

Though Seattle was home, he couldn't help but like the midday heat of the desert. And though he first thought the landscape was bare and lifeless, he was quickly learning to appreciate the stark beauty of it.

He had so many questions to ask, but it was impossible to talk with the noise of the wind and the Jeep's engine. Instead, he made a careful study of the woman he'd now call "boss."

He was usually more attracted to blondes and had dated the occasional redhead. But Sofie was something different. She was beautiful, but she was also tough and determined, resilient and focused. This was a woman who knew exactly what she wanted in life.

By the time Sofie pulled the Jeep into a parking spot in front of the Holman Public Library, he'd jumped out and circled around to help her out.

"You don't have to do that," she said.

"I'm hoping to be your right-hand man," he said. "So I need to make myself indispensable."

She reached behind his seat and pulled out a backpack, slinging it over her shoulder. Then he took her hand and steadied her as she hopped out of the Jeep. As they strolled up to the front doors, he realized that her limp was more pronounced. He took the backpack from her and placed his hand on the small of her back. At this point, he was willing to use any excuse to touch her again.

"My hip gets stiff if I stay in one position too long," she explained. "Like when I'm driving."

Cameron wanted to ask her about the injury. But he knew she'd tell him when she was ready. "Maybe I should do the driving from now on," he offered. "Then you can move around a little more."

She smiled at him and he felt the warmth right down to his bones. "That would be nice," she said.

When they got inside the library, Sofie headed directly for the reading tables. She opened the backpack and pulled out a small laptop, then signed on to the internet. "Cameron Quinn," she said, typing his name into a Google search. "Seattle, Washington."

He grinned as a list of hits came up on her screen. "Try this one," he said, pointing to the website for Quinn Yachtworks. "I designed this then hired someone to code it all." He pointed to a picture. "See, that's me and my three brothers and my grandfather."

"So you are who you say you are," she said, glancing over at him. He couldn't help but notice the reluctant smile that teased at the corners of her mouth.

He reached over and clicked on his bio, and another screen popped up, this with more pictures. She looked at them carefully. "You're very..."

"Handsome?" he teased.

"Accomplished," she said. "So explain to me again why you're looking for a low-paying job in Vulture Creek, New Mexico?"

"My grandfather owns the Yachtworks. He has to decide who to put in charge when he retires. He wants us all to explore our options before we commit to the company for good."

"Couldn't you figure that out in Seattle?"

"Yeah. But you don't know my grandfather. I think he wanted us to see a totally different lifestyle. He sent me to Vulture Creek because I had a childhood dream to be a paleontologist. I guess he thought there were dinosaur bones around here."

"There are," she said. "My uncle owns a ranch west of Vulture Creek. He has a wash that's filled with all kinds of old bones. We used to dig around there when we were kids."

"Really? I'd like to see that."

"I could show you," she murmured. "There are also a lot of Anasazi sites around here. You should see those, as well."

Cameron reached out and pulled the laptop in front of him. "Can I do a Google search on you?"

"If you have any questions, you can just ask me."

She closed the computer. "I'll tell you anything you want to know."

"All right. How long have you been a private investigator?"

"About a year and a half."

"What did you do before that?"

"I was on the police force in Albuquerque for four years," she said. "I worked patrol at first, then transferred over to Narcotics. I was undercover until I got hurt. Now I'm working for my uncle until I can pass the physical and get back on the force."

"How did you get hurt?"

Sofie turned to meet his gaze. "I made a stupid mistake." For a long moment, she just stared into his eyes, as if trying to read his reaction. But all Cam could think about was leaning forward and touching his lips to hers.

He wanted to kiss her. He already knew how it would feel, the surge of desire that would wash over him, the heat that would snake through his bloodstream. He hadn't found much time for a social life in the past few months, and he was feeling the need for physical contact.

Cameron didn't usually spend a lot of thought on the pursuit of women. He was of the belief that when he really needed companionship, a woman would appear in his life. The philosophy had worked out well for the most part. There were periods in his past when he'd lost himself in the pursuit of pleasure and other times when he'd go months without any social contact with the opposite sex, being so preoccupied with work.

It had been a while since he'd shared his bed, Cameron thought to himself. He'd been involved with a new hull design at work, and it had taken every last minute of his time to perfect it before they'd put it into production. Now would be a perfect time to indulge.

Yet every instinct he possessed told him to take his time. Sofie Reyes wasn't the kind of female one could simply bed and then abandon. She was cautious and guarded, and he wasn't sure how to break down the walls between them. He saw something else in her—a vulnerability, a fragility, that warned him to proceed carefully. He would need to control his impulses and school his desires until she wanted him as much as he wanted her.

"Any more questions?" she asked.

Cameron shook his head.

"I have one more," Sofie said in a soft voice. Her gaze drifted down to his mouth.

"What is it?"

"You have to be completely honest," she said. "Can you do that?"

Cameron nodded. "Ask away."

"What are you thinking about? Right now? What's running through your mind?"

He paused. Was he really prepared to tell the truth? If he did, there was every chance he'd feel compelled to turn thought into action. "I'm not sure I should—"

"Answer my question," she said.

"Honestly?" Cameron cleared his throat. "I was thinking about what it would be like to kiss you. Not that I had any intention of trying to kiss you. It just crossed my mind. And hey, you asked for honesty."

She didn't seem at all surprised by his reply. The only reaction he saw was a quick blink of her eyes and a barely perceptible gasp.

"I'm not sure that would be wise," Sofie said.

Cameron looked around, taking in their surroundings. "Not here. And not now. But maybe sometime. In the future."

"When?" Sofie asked.

He shrugged. "I don't know. You can't really plan things like that. They're much better when they come spontaneously, don't you think?"

Sofie nodded. "We should go. We have a lot of work to do today." She stood up and gathered her things, putting her computer back into her backpack.

"Just tell me what to do," he said. "I'm ready."

She pulled a file folder from her pack and handed it to him. "You can read this." She started for the door.

Curious, Cam took the folder and opened it as they walked. A black-and-white photo of a middle-aged man smiled back at him—the kind of guy that everyone loved, everyone trusted. "He's a politician?"

She shook her head. "No. But he knows a lot of politicians. His name is Walter Fredericks. He's a real-estate broker and developer around Albuquerque. He owns most of the property in Vulture Creek, including Millie's diner, plus land in almost every little town between Albuquerque and Gallup. He's very well connected."

"Does Millie know you're investigating him?"

"No," Sofie said. "He's got a mistress in Vulture Creek. He's got her set up in a nice little ranch outside town. I'm pretty sure he's been paying her expenses with kickbacks he's getting on some of his construction projects. And the people in his office are aware of this. I also suspect that there's something else going on. He does a lot of business out of the local strip club, which seems to be the regular gathering place for the criminal element in these parts."

When they got to the Jeep, she got in behind the wheel and Cameron slipped into the passenger seat. "He spends the morning at his office in Albuquerque, drives out to Vulture Creek and has lunch at the Bunny Shack most days, then spends the afternoon with his mistress. He heads back to Albuquerque at about three and has dinner with his wife."

"You said he buys and sells real estate? Maybe I could mention that I'm looking to make some investments in the area."

"That's not a bad idea," she said, nodding.

"It's a good idea," he said. "I could have lunch at the Bunny Shack tomorrow. Chat him up."

"We'll have to work on a cover story for you. Why would a yacht designer from Seattle want to buy land in Vulture Creek?"

"I'm looking to start over. Someplace where it doesn't rain every day. I'm about to come into some big money when my grandfather sells the family business and I've always been interested in paleontology. I really don't have to do anything but tell the truth."

"All right, you are good at this. The closer you stay to the truth, the easier it is. But you need to get personal information out of him without seeming too nosy. Steer the talk toward women. You're alone in town. You're lonely."

"But I'm not lonely," he said.

"You're going to have to pretend. I need to know as much as I can about this woman. Her name. Where he met her. How long he's known her. What their arrangement is."

"Maybe I should wear a wire," he said.

Sofie laughed. "A wire?"

"Yeah. To record our conversation. That way you know exactly what he says and I don't have to remember it all."

She turned on the ignition and pulled the Jeep out of the library parking lot. "We'll practice before we throw you in the deep end."

"So, I have the job?" Cameron asked.

"Yes, you have the job. For now. But only as long as you do everything exactly as I say. Agreed?"

"Agreed," Cameron said. "We should probably discuss compensation. I'm going to have to find a place to stay."

"I'll take care of your expenses," she said. "If you do a good job, I'll give you a small stipend. And if we get what we need, then there'll be a bonus for you."

"All right," he said. "I can live with that."

She smiled. "Don't worry, I plan to get my money's worth out of you," Sofie teased.

CAMERON STARED AT himself in the mirror, nodding his head. "I like this one," he muttered, tugging at the sleeves of the pale blue work shirt. "It feels good. The sleeves are long enough."

Once they'd found a hat, Sofie realized that Cameron would need a few long-sleeved shirts to protect his arms from the sun. All he'd brought along were dress shirts and T-shirts. But she hadn't prepared herself for the fitting-room ordeal of watching him actually try the shirts on.

"That is a nice one," she said. "It fits...well." Sofie swallowed hard. He had such a beautiful body—long limbs, a finely muscled chest, broad shoulders. "And it will keep you from getting sunburned."

"The heat down here is pretty intense," he agreed as he unbuttoned the shirt. "Not like Seattle. That's a city made for Irish skin." He grabbed her hand and held it next to his. "I'm downright pasty next to you."

She shrugged "I owe half of that to my Mexican father and the other half to my Hopi mother."

"It's a nice combination," he murmured. "They did a good job."

Her gaze skimmed over the naked width of his back as he slipped out of the shirt and handed it to her. Sofie's fingers trembled as she fought the urge to touch him. "I—I should probably put the roof on my Jeep. That would help with the sun."

Cameron pulled on another shirt, this one a deep garnet color. "How about this? Good for lunch at the Bunny Shack."

She watched as Cameron toyed with the mother-of-pearl buttons on the pockets. He did look good in the deep red. It set off his dark hair and impossibly blue eyes. "The girls there are going to love you. They'll be all over you before you even sit down."

"You think so?" he asked, frowning.

"You need to be careful. They've been around—they know how to read men, how to get exactly what they want from a guy. And they have really good radar. They're going to know if you're hiding something or lying to them."

"I can handle it. I got you to hire me, didn't I?"

"I could always fire you," she said. "You're still on probation."

"You have too much invested in me to fire me. You bought me lunch."

And she was about to pay for his new wardrobe. In truth, Sofie was curious about their future together as partners. As she'd worked her way up through the ranks at the SFPD, she'd always had male partners, but they'd been more like brothers or uncles. She'd never once considered indulging in a sexual affair with one of them.

But that's all she could think about with Cameron. Sure, they'd work together on the case. But she was much more interested in what was going to happen outside of the workday.

Cameron grabbed the straw cowboy hat they'd chosen and put it on his head. "What do you think? Can I pass for a local?"

She laughed, then readjusted the hat on his head. "No. Not at all. There aren't any men like you living within a hundred miles of Vulture Creek."

"No?"

"You're just too pretty. Look at that face."

He shook his head. "What does that even mean?" His voice was soft, distracted.

"Oh, come on," she teased. "Don't pretend that you don't know what you do to women. A guy like you doesn't go through life not realizing the advantages you have because of your looks."

Cameron glanced over at her. "I look like my brothers."

Sofie groaned inwardly. He was the most dangerous of men, the kind of guy who didn't even have a clue as to the devastating effect he had on women.

"My mother used to tell me I was handsome. She'd dress us all up for church on Sunday, then line us up and go on and on about how handsome her boys were. After she was gone, I didn't like to hear it. It would always bring back that memory."

"I'm sorry," she said.

He reached out and grabbed her hand, giving it a squeeze. "No, it's all right. I haven't thought about that for such a long time. It's kind of a nice memory."

"My dad always used to tell me I was pretty. I was his princess. And he'd tell my brothers that they were strong and clever." Sofie sighed. "I wanted to be strong and clever. I didn't want to be a princess."

"Is that why you became a cop?"

"Yeah, I think I had something to prove. To my dad and my brothers. And now that I'm not a cop anymore, I have even more to prove."

"What if you're never a cop again?" Cameron asked.

She closed her eyes and shook her head. "I can't think about that. It's all I know how to do."

"That's not true. I thought all I was good at was designing boats. But since I stepped off that bus, I realize that I just haven't considered anything else."

"You think you want to be a private investigator now?"

Cameron laughed. "No. But I'm not my job." He grabbed her hand and pulled her next to him, their gazes meeting in the reflection of the mirror. "I haven't known you long, but I can tell you the woman in that mirror could ride a bicycle to the moon if she decided that's what she wanted to do."

"You're a nice guy, Cameron Quinn."

"I'm handsome and nice," he said. "And strippers will love me."

She met his gaze and smiled. He didn't say much, but when he did, they were words she could believe in. She could trust Cameron to tell her the truth. "You're handsome and nice and honest."

Maybe she should start to consider other options, Sofie mused. What if she never got back to form? So much of her life had been spent trying to prove something to her father and brothers—that she was good enough to be one of them. Maybe it was time to find out who she really was.

"And you're just about the most beautiful thing I've ever seen," he said.

His words startled Sofie at first. It had been a long time since a man had noticed her. Since her accident, she'd put up a wall around herself to ward off any interested parties. The scars from her injury had faded, but there were other scars buried much deeper.

Could she trust herself again? Could she imagine a life that didn't include the career she'd dreamed about since she was a little girl? Her friends had wanted to be princesses and fairies, then movie stars and supermodels, and finally wives and mothers. Through it all, Sofie had wanted the uniform, the badge, the power to make a difference in the world.

Sofie stepped away from the mirror, but Cameron caught her hand and pulled her back, placing him in front of her. She couldn't be beautiful and be taken seriously. Beauty meant weakness, not strength.

His hands smoothed over her shoulders and down her arms. Sofie's heart slammed in her chest and she couldn't catch her breath. This was crazy! She'd always been known for keeping her cool under pressure, but now she was having trouble holding it together, simply because of some guy. Some handsome, sexy, irresistible guy.

"I—I really don't have time for this," she murmured. If this was the way the next few weeks were going to go, then she'd be lucky if she got anything done. "The sooner I close this case, the sooner I can get back to—" She cursed softly in Spanish, then turned to him and wagged her finger in his face. "You need to stop distracting me."

They stared at each other for a long moment, and then, in a heartbeat, Cameron took her face between his hands and kissed her.

It was brief, barely a touch, but as she pulled back, a tiny gasp slipped from her lips. Sofie's knees felt weak and she reached out, pressing her hand against his chest for balance. "I'll wait for you outside," she muttered, grabbing her hat.

When she'd put some distance between them, Sofie leaned back against the wall and tried to calm her racing pulse. She'd been waiting for something like this, for the chance to indulge her fantasies. And now that the moment had arrived, she wasn't sure what to do about it.

This was her problem. For the most part, she was like her mother—calm, rational, self-controlled. But every now and then, her father's fiery personality showed itself in her, and she did something so rash and impulsive she wanted to slap herself. It was that half of her nature that usually got her in trouble.

Cameron joined her at the counter, and Sofie paid for the clothes before they both walked out into the afternoon heat. A shiver skittered down her spine as Cameron's shoulder brushed against hers. Her thoughts returned to the kiss.

Why hadn't she just allowed it to go on a little longer? It had happened so quickly, she wasn't even sure it was a kiss. Maybe it had been just incidental contact. The dressing room was small, the mood a bit tense and—

No, it had definitely been a kiss. And it was something they ought to discuss. But if they talked about it, it might happen again. And if it happened again, Sofie wasn't sure she'd want to stop things so quickly.

"What's next, boss?" Cameron said. "Should we go see if Walter is at the strip club?"

Sofie pulled the car keys from her pocket. "We're too late for today. If he follows his pattern, he'll be there tomorrow." She stopped and faced him. "About that—that—"

"Kiss?" he asked.

She nodded. "I'm not sure that's the most productive use of our time."

Her breath was soft and shallow, and Sofie was sure he could hear her heart pounding in her chest. Had any man ever made her feel this way? Her fingers and toes had gone numb and her head was spinning.

"You're the boss," Cameron said.

"Yes," Sofie replied. "Yes, I am." And though it was easy to say the words, she had the distinct impression that when it came to kissing, Cameron was definitely in charge.

CAMERON HAD THOUGHT the roads on the bus route had been desolate, but as they drove out into the desert, he realized that he hadn't really appreciated the meaning of the word.

The land was flat all around them, and then suddenly, it would change, with rocky outcroppings appearing out of nowhere. In the distance, snow-covered mountains outlined the horizon. Everywhere he looked, the land was dry. But the terrain he'd once thought of as colorless suddenly showed a vast range of vibrant golds and browns.

"Where are we going?"

Sofie shrugged. "Home."

"To your place?"

"No," she shouted. "To my uncle's place. I've been staying there while I've been working on the case."

"The ranch with the dinosaur bones?" Cameron asked.

"That's it," she said.

Cam grinned. It wasn't the worst thing in the world to be driving through the desert with a beautiful, exotic private investigator. He watched as a strand of hair escaped from her braid and fluttered around her face.

She glanced over at him, catching him staring again, and he grudgingly looked away. "I feel like I'm on the moon," he shouted. "This land is so different from anything I know."

"I hear it rains a lot in Seattle," she said.

"And here the sun never seems to stop. I haven't seen a cloud all day." He looked up at the sky. "Does it ever rain?"

She shook her head. "Occasionally." Sofie pointed to an upcoming intersection. "Turn right."

"I'm really beginning to like this job," he said.

"It's not always like this. Sometimes I just sit in my car watching a dark house. Last month I spent two days in a Laundromat watching a restaurant across the street. I did the same load of laundry fifteen times."

"I'm liking it," he said.

"We haven't done anything yet."

"What made you choose this kind of work? Isn't it a little unusual for a woman?"

"My dad's a cop and I have five older brothers and they all work in law enforcement. Three are cops, one works for the ATF, and one for the FBI."

Cam leaned back in his seat. "Wow. I guess I better watch myself."

"If I don't scare men away with my sparkling personality, then my brothers do it for me."

"You actually think I'm going to believe that you scare men away?" Cameron said.

"It's usually the limp," she said. "Most men don't like women who are…damaged."

Cameron gasped at her statement. Cursing beneath his breath, he pulled the Jeep over to the side of the road and threw it into Park. "That's the most ridiculous thing I've ever heard."

She shrugged. "It's the truth. I'm not feeling sorry for myself. I'm just being realistic."

Cameron wasn't sure how to respond. How could any man look at Sofie Reyes and consider her damaged? "Has a guy said that to you?"

"No, but you can see it in their expressions. I saw it in yours when you looked at me at the diner."

Cameron remembered the uneasy feeling he'd had when he'd noticed her limp. But it hadn't stopped him from finding her attractive or sexy or intriguing.

"Maybe we should just talk about this now," Sofie said. "I know you have questions. Just go ahead and ask them."

"I don't need to know," he said.

"You stopped the Jeep," she countered. "Come on. If we're working together, we can at least be honest with each other. Ask me how it happened."

Cameron gripped the steering wheel with white-knuckled hands. Though he'd been curious, in the end, he really didn't care. Whatever had happened was in the past. And it wasn't going to change how he felt about Sofie. He was more interested in the here and now, the desire that was racing through him, the urge he had to yank her into his arms and kiss her.

"All right," Sofie said, "If you're not going to ask, then I'll tell you." She sat silently for a moment, as if trying to put order to her thoughts. "My mother once said, be careful what you wish for—it might come true. I never really understood why that would be a bad thing. And then my dreams came true. I was a cop, I'd been picked for an undercover task force, I was on my way to getting my detective's shield, and I was ready to break open a huge case. I was exactly where I wanted to be."

"What happened?"

"I took a risk. I got into a car with a suspect, and the next thing I remember, I woke up in intensive care. We got into a police chase and they didn't know I was in the car. He died and I lived. I was in the hospital for three months and then rehab after that. After the accident, I couldn't pass the physical and didn't want to sit at a desk all day long. So as soon as I could get around, I went to work for my uncle. He used to be a cop but he's a P.I. now."

"I don't think you're damaged," he said.

"You don't have to live with losing your dreams."

He leaned close, pressing his palm against her cheek. Then, without thinking, Cameron brushed his lips across hers. "There are a lot of other dreams out there, Sofie," he murmured. "You just need to go look for them."

He saw the tears flooding her eyes, and he turned away, upset that he'd brought her to this emotional state. "I think you're a pretty amazing woman. I've only known you a day. Just think how I'll feel after a week."

"You'll want to catch the first bus back to Seattle," she said.

He steered the Jeep back onto the road. "You really have five brothers?"

Sofie smiled. "I do. And they insist on interrogating any man that kisses me. So you better stop that right now, or you're going to be in big trouble."

"You think they could take me?" he asked.

"Hell, I could take you," Sofie said.

"I'd like you to try," he challenged.

The mood between them shifted again, and Cameron had to wonder why it was so easy to talk to Sofie. He'd never been much for conversation with other women. He usually hated idle chitchat. But with Sofie, it was like a game between them, a game he was coming to enjoy.

"I can take care of myself," Sofie shouted.

Cameron arched his brow. The thought of being overpowered by such a beautiful creature created a delicious fantasy in his head. But his thoughts were interrupted by a loud bang.

The Jeep jerked and then swerved on the rough asphalt road. Cameron gripped the steering wheel tightly as he slowed to a stop, a plume of dust rising from the skidding tires.

"Flat tire," Sofie muttered, cursing beneath her breath in Spanish.

Cameron chuckled softly. "I suppose the auto club doesn't come out this far. No worries. I know how to change a tire."

Sofie jumped out of the Jeep. "So do I. These desert roads are notoriously bad on tires." She strode to the back of the vehicle and squatted down to examine the rear wheel. She straightened, then kicked the tire. "It was brand-new."

As Cameron stood behind her, his attention was caught by the curve of her backside as she shoved her hands in the pockets of her jeans. Though she wore simple work clothes, there was no disputing that they hid an incredible combination of curves. And the more time he spent with her, the more curious he became about the body beneath.

Cameron sighed softly. This was not the time to be thinking about seducing his boss, especially one who probably knew how to kill him with one quick chop to the throat. And yet he couldn't seem to help himself.

Sofie spun around, catching him staring again. "Are you going to just stand there with your mouth hanging open, or are you going to help me?"

"Help," he said, quickly moving past her. Cameron noticed that she carried two spares in the cargo compartment of the Jeep. He found the tire iron and jack next to the spares and pulled both of them out. "Why don't you just let me take care of this?" Cameron said.

"I can help," she replied. She reached for one of the tires and tried to pull it out of the back of the Jeep. Cameron dropped the tire iron and jack. "Here, let me get that."

"I can get it," she said stubbornly.

He reached around her. "It's heavy. It would be easier if you opened the tailgate."

"I can get it," she insisted.

But their arms and feet got tangled, and when Sofie finally pulled the tire over the edge of the cargo compartment, the weight of it knocked them both off balance. He grabbed her waist and yanked her out of the way as the tire fell on the dusty road.

They tumbled back onto the hard ground, Cameron taking the weight of her body in the fall. She ended up lying on top of him, his hands spanning her waist. Their eyes met and Cameron was afraid to speak, knowing that it might break this strange spell that had fallen over them both.

Hesitantly, she leaned closer, her lips just inches from his. And then closer again. He drew one more ragged breath then slipped his hand gently around her nape. He waited, hoping she'd take his touch as an invitation to go further. And when she did, the breath rushed out of him as her lips met his.

This time, the kiss was filled with all the repressed desire that they'd both tried to deny. She surrendered her body to his touch as Cameron explored her mouth more deeply. His tongue delved inside the sweet warmth and she didn't resist. He wrapped his arms around her waist and pulled her closer, rolling her onto the ground beneath him. Slowly, his hands smoothed along her hip. He pulled her thigh up along the length of his leg.

She drew back and he saw the desire clouding her gaze. As much as she'd maintained a careful distance since they'd met, Cameron suspected that there was an attraction that she'd been fighting as hard as he had. He smiled, reaching out to cup her cheek in his hand. "That was nice," he murmured.

Sofie nodded. "Yes," she replied.

He leaned in for another kiss and they lost themselves again. Her hands clutched at the front of his shirt, holding on to him as they rolled around in the dirt.

And then, as quick as it had begun, she stopped and yanked him upright, scrambling to her feet. She pulled him up with her. A moment later, she brought her foot down on the ground where they'd just been lying. "Scorpion," she murmured.

Cameron gasped. "What? Where?"

"Under my boot. You have to be careful around here. In the morning, shake out your shoes and clothes. Don't walk around barefoot."

"Are they poisonous?"

"They won't kill you. But the bite is pretty painful." She dusted off her clothes then strode to the spot where the tire had come to rest. She hefted it up and rolled it toward the back of the Jeep, as if she was glad to have something else to focus on.

By the time they got the tire fixed, it was all Cameron could do to keep his hands off Sofie. The last kiss just hadn't been enough to satisfy his curiosity. He wanted more time to touch her, to learn exactly what made her sigh with pleasure.

After they'd stowed the flat tire, Cameron helped Sofie back into the Jeep then got behind the wheel. As they roared down the road, a plume of dust blossoming behind them, he chuckled to himself. He could honestly say he'd never meet a woman quite like Sofie Reyes. She was a mass of contradictions, soft yet tough, beautiful yet filled with a steely determination. Vulnerable yet resilient.

When he'd been given the bus ticket to Vulture Creek, Cameron couldn't have imagined anything like this happening to him. But now that he was here, it was the only place in the world he wanted to be.

3

"WHERE THE HELL did you find him?"

Sofie stood in the middle of the kitchen, her brother Tony striding back and forth in front of her. She hadn't expected to find him at the ranch, but he'd come out to check on her after he'd talked to their uncle about her case.

"I met him at Millie's in Vulture Creek. He was looking for a job and I needed help with Fredericks."

"You need help tailing a cheating husband. Hell, Sof, you can do that in your sleep."

"I can't just walk into the Bunny Shack and see who he's meeting at lunch. But I can send Cameron in."

"Cameron?" Tony asked. "What kind of name is that?"

"I believe it's Irish."

"Irish?"

"Yeah, his last name is Quinn. He's from Seattle."

"Why are you even doing this, Sof? You don't

need to work. You have your disability pay. You could go back to school. Or help Mama out at the gallery. You were always pretty good at making those pots. Chasing some scumbag around the desert is no kind of job for you."

"This is what I know how to do. And I can't spend every waking hour on rehab. Maybe I don't move as well as I used to, but I'm getting better. I'm still a great investigator. And I'm going to get back on the force. So don't you dare tell me what I can and can't do."

"Well, I've got a few days off. I can help you. You don't need to drag in a stray."

"He's not a stray. He's smart and he needs the work. And a place to stay."

"He's not staying here," Tony said.

"I told him he could stay in the Airstream."

Tony shook his head. "No, no, no. We're not putting up some stranger."

"He's helping me with my work," she said. "So this is the way it's going to be. And this isn't your house, so you can't dictate who can stay and who can't." She glanced around the kitchen. "Now, what do we have for dinner? I'm going to have to feed him. That's part of the deal."

"What else did you include in the deal?" he asked.

Sofie slapped him on the shoulder, then crossed to the refrigerator and opened the door. "Got anything interesting?"

"You're not going to give him my birthday tamales. Mom made those for me."

She pulled out the pan and peeked under the crumpled foil. "Don't worry, I'll make you more."

"No!" Tony said, reaching for the pan.

She evaded his grasp and ran to the other side of the table. "They're just tamales. I promise, as soon as I get back to Albuquerque I'll make a whole batch."

"No!" he said as he chased her to the other side of the kitchen. "Give those back. They're not yours, they're—" Tony froze, his gaze fixed on the screen door. She turned to find Cameron watching them.

"Hi." Sofie crossed the room and opened the door. "Come on in."

Cameron reluctantly stepped inside, shifting his gaze between her and Tony. His hair was wet and he was dressed in a faded T-shirt and jeans. "Sorry, I didn't mean to interrupt. I was just looking for something to drink. Something cold."

"Cameron, this is my brother Antonio. We call him Tony. Tony, this is Cameron Quinn, my new… my new assistant investigator."

Reluctantly, Tony held out his hand. "Hi," he muttered.

"Nice to meet you, Tony. I didn't expect to meet any of Sofie's brothers. Are you one of the policemen?"

Her brother seemed surprised by Cameron's friendly nature. Though the tension in the room was obvious, Cameron had managed to defuse it in a matter of seconds. "ATF," Tony said. "And what do you do when you're not helping my sister?"

"I design sailboats," Cameron said. "Yachts, actually."

"What the hell are you doing in the middle of the desert?"

"Good question, long story. I wouldn't want to bore you."

"I'm going to get you some clean sheets," Sofie said. "I'll bring them out in a bit." She handed him the pan of tamales then grabbed a couple beers from the fridge. "Take these out. We can eat on the picnic table."

Cameron nodded as he took the pan. "Tony, it was nice meeting you. Are you going to have dinner with us?"

"No," Tony said. "Enjoy the tamales."

Sofie and Tony watched him leave, and the moment he was out of earshot, Tony groaned. "Okay, now I get it. Of course. It makes all the sense in the world."

"What is that supposed to mean?"

"Come on, Sofie, give me a break. It's pretty clear why you brought his guy home. And I don't approve. Neither would Ma and Pop. So take him back to town and tell him to find his own place to stay."

"I have every right to have a guest."

"A guest? Is that what you're calling him?"

"There's nothing going on between us."

"Oh, no? Then wipe that goofy look off your

face." He shook his finger at her. "I'm not going to let you compromise your virtue over some stranger."

Sofie laughed. "I'm twenty-eight years old, Tony. My virtue was compromised a long time ago."

He opened his mouth, then snapped it shut, shaking his head. "I don't want to hear this. I owe it to Ma and Pop to see that nothing bad happens to you."

"Don't you think that's a bit hypocritical? You spend at least a few nights a week with Arianna Lopez. Maybe I should be concerned about your virtue. Or perhaps hers?"

"That is none of your business," he said. "Get rid of him."

"No. He's staying. And you can stay out of my business. I'm perfectly capable of running my own sex life."

Tony clapped his hands to his ears. "I don't want to hear this. La la la la la. I'm not listening."

Sofie grabbed a jar of salsa from the refrigerator, then pushed open the screen door and stepped outside. Her sex life. The words had just popped out of her mouth. Was that what she was hoping for? She hadn't been with a man since the accident, and yet she could easily imagine falling into bed with Cameron.

She drew in a deep breath as a shiver skittered down her spine. Suddenly, her scars didn't matter. She wasn't afraid anymore. Had enough time finally passed? Or was this simply because of Cameron himself?

For some strange reason, she trusted him. And after spending four years as a cop, Sofie didn't trust anyone other than her parents and her brothers. She smiled to herself. It felt good to let someone in, to forget everything that had happened and just enjoy the moment.

When she got back to the trailer, Cameron was sitting at the picnic table, munching on a tamale, his expression somber.

"Maybe it's just me, but these things are kind of tough."

"You don't eat the husk," she said. "And they're supposed to be warmed up. You put a bit of salsa on them. This is my mom's roasted-corn salsa."

He glanced down at the half-eaten tamale. "Oh. I guess I should have waited for instructions."

Sofie picked up the pan and carried it to the trailer. "Come on, I'll explain everything." She set the tamales on the counter next to the microwave, and he stood behind her, watching over her shoulder. A moment later, his hands circled her waist and gently turned her to face him.

She held her breath, waiting for him to kiss her again. When he picked her up and set her on the edge of the counter, a tiny cry of surprise escaped her lips. Cameron stepped between her legs, pulled her against his hips until she had no choice but to hang on to him or fall to the floor.

"What are you doing?" she murmured, her gaze drifting down to his mouth.

"Finishing something I started earlier," he said. He leaned forward and kissed her, his lips gently teasing. His fingers drifted down to the front of her shirt and he pulled it aside to press his mouth to her bare shoulder.

She closed her eyes and drew a slow breath, waiting for his lips to follow his fingers. But he didn't kiss her again. Instead, he slowly pushed her shirt over her shoulders, bunching it behind her. Sofie gripped the edge of the counter and watched him as he drew his hand across her chest.

A moment later, he slipped his hand beneath her breast, cupping the soft flesh under the fabric of her camisole. His gaze met hers as he teased at her nipple through the layers of her clothes. She hadn't been touched like this in so long, Sofie had forgotten how exhilarating, how thrilling it all was. Every nerve in her body felt as if it were alive, vibrating with anticipation. And with every shift of his touch, she wanted more, his mouth on her skin, his hands against her flesh.

She'd frozen out all these wonderful feelings, and now that they'd flooded back all at once, Sofie wasn't sure what to do with them. She wanted to throw herself into his arms and laugh; she wanted to crawl into his bed and cry. Every emotion that she'd ever had in her life was pulsing through her body in one wonderful, horrible, confusing mess.

"I've been thinking about this all day," he said.

"All day?" she asked.

"Since I saw you eat that piece of pie. I was intrigued."

"About pie?" Sofie sighed. "You scare me a little bit."

"Why?"

"I don't know if I can do this. It's not that easy." She forced a smile. "I mean, it is easy. It's like riding a bike. But everything that comes with it… It can get complicated. Promise me that it won't get complicated."

"I'll promise anything you want," he said. "But we're just kissing and touching and…messing around a little. It's all just harmless fun."

"We barely know each other," she whispered. "We just met this morning."

"What do you want to know?" Cameron asked. "You told me about your life. I'll tell you about mine. Ask me anything."

She smiled at him. "All right." She thought about her question for a long moment, but she felt foolish asking him anything personal. She didn't want to know about ex-girlfriends or when he lost his virginity or why he seemed so obsessed with kissing her. "How is it that you don't know how to eat a tamale?"

He blinked in surprise. "That's what you want to know?"

She nodded. "I mean, tamales are just about the most perfect food and—"

"Except for pie," he said.

"Well, yes, except for pie. But don't they have tamales in Seattle?"

"I'm sure they do, but I've never had one. I guess I've led a sheltered life. But I am counting on you to introduce me to these things. So far, I've eaten tacos and fajitas."

"That's not real Mexican food," she said. "My mother makes the best mole poblano. She learned from my grandmother Reyes. It's a sauce you put on chicken or pork. She cooks it for hours and hours, and it has about thirty ingredients in it."

"What can you cook?" he asked.

"Chile Rellenos. And I can make tamales. But I'm really not much of a cook." She forced a smile. What was she doing? Here was a man dying to seduce her, to drag her to the bed, and she was bragging about her prowess in the kitchen. She *should* be showing him what she could accomplish in the bedroom. "What would you feed me if I came to your house?"

"You mean Irish food? It's not nearly as tasty as Mexican food. My grandfather is a pretty decent cook, though. Every Sunday we'd have a big supper together. He'd make the things he ate as a child—bacon and cabbage, meat pies, colcannon, boxty. Lots of potatoes. Our potatoes are kind of like your tortillas. We put them in every dish." He paused. "Are we really talking about food?"

Sofie reached for the hem of his T-shirt and tugged it over his head. Then she ran her hands across his chest, her fingers skimming over smooth skin and hard muscle. "I like talking to you."

"I like talking to you."

She smiled. "So, you wanna make out?"

"Yeah," he said, nodding. "But I don't sleep with girls that I barely know."

"Then I think we ought to get to know each other a little better." She gave him a winsome smile. "We have the most beautiful sunsets in this part of New Mexico. Why don't I heat up these tamales and you open the beers, and we'll go outside and watch the show?"

He drew her hand to his lips and pressed a kiss on her fingertips. "I think that sounds like a good plan."

If it was meant to happen, then it would happen, Sofie mused. For a man like Cameron, it would most definitely be worth the wait.

A COOL BREEZE BLEW through the louvered windows of the trailer, rustling the leaves of the cottonwood tree outside. To Cameron's surprise, the heat from the day had dissipated at sunset, and darkness brought a more comfortable temperature.

Cameron stretched out on the sofa bed in the Airstream and turned his attention back to the paperback he'd brought along for the bus ride. He'd have to make a point of buying a few more books, especially if he was going to be spending his nights alone.

After watching the sunset and enjoying a dinner of tamales, eaten on the picnic table outside, Sofie had bid him a quick good-night. She left him for her own bed, warning him that they'd discuss their next move over breakfast the next morning at Millie's.

Cameron didn't feel like sleeping. Instead, his mind was occupied with thoughts of his new boss. Though he did technically work for her, Cameron wasn't going to let that get in the way of his attraction. There was some invisible force that had drawn them to each other, that made intimacy almost inevitable. He wasn't going to deny it, and he was pretty sure she didn't intend to, either.

But how long would they ignore their desires before they finally gave in? Would this become a game between them, or would they both admit that they wanted the same thing?

A knock sounded on the trailer door, and Cameron pushed up on his elbow. Maybe he wouldn't have to wait after all, he mused. But it wasn't Sofie at the door. Her brother Tony stepped inside.

"Hi," Cameron said, swinging his legs over the edge of the sofa to sit.

"I didn't wake you, did I?" he asked. "I meant to talk to you earlier, but I noticed you and Sofie were…"

"No, I was awake," Cameron said. "What's up?"

Tony leaned against the edge of the table, his arms crossed over his broad chest. "How much has she told you?"

Cam shrugged. "I don't know. I guess she's told me most of it. I know she worked for the Albuquerque Police Department and that she was hurt on the job. And that she's working as a P.I. until she can get her old job back."

"She's not going back to police work," Tony said. "She should have never been doing that in the first place. She's got this crazy need to compete with us. She takes too many risks and doesn't think about the consequences."

Cameron frowned. "Sofie can make her own decisions."

"Right," Tony said. "I know you're probably just passing through and you've got a whole other life somewhere else, but just make sure you don't leave a mess here when you go. You know what I mean?"

Cameron shook his head. "Not exactly."

"Sofie. She's been hurt before, by a guy who was a lot like you. A guy she trusted. A guy who thought she could make her own decisions. He was wrong. And you are, too."

Cameron nodded. "Okay," he said.

Tony pushed to his feet. "If you're going to work with her, make damn sure you watch her back. We almost lost her once. It would kill my mother if anything happened to her again."

"I'll do that." Cameron nodded. "You don't have to worry."

Tony pointed an accusing finger at him. "You fuck up and I'll personally feed you to the coyotes." With that, he walked out of the trailer.

Cameron wandered to the door and stared out at

the night. A wash of light from the back porch illuminated the house. He drew a deep breath and let it out slowly, listening for the sounds of utter desolation. In the distance, a coyote howled, the sound sending a shiver down his spine.

Sure, her brother would be protective. But Sofie was a grown woman. She could make her own decisions. He slipped on his boat shoes and walked out behind the trailer, staring up into the night sky. He'd never seen so many stars.

There was something about this land, something he found so raw and elemental, something that seemed to strip away his old life and leave him with nothing but the man he truly was. Had his grandfather known when he sent him here that this would be the perfect place? Here, he could clear his head and reevaluate his choices. This place gave him nothing but time and space to think—and to feel.

The truth was he'd never delved very deeply into his own emotional life. It had always been easier to push that away and to approach everything in a logical, dispassionate manner. Unfortunately, he'd spent his adult life not really feeling anything at all.

In this severe and empty place, he felt as if the veneer he'd so successfully hidden behind would crumble away, revealing the real man underneath. Cameron drew a deep breath and let it out slowly. Who would he be when this was all over? Would he be ready to go back to his former life, or would he begin all over again?

"What are you doing out here?"

Cameron slowly turned to see Sofie's silhouette in the darkness. She wore a pale cotton nightdress that blew in the breeze, fluttering around her bare legs. Her hair was free of its braid and tumbled across her shoulders. "Thinking," he said.

"About?"

"Lots of different things." He shrugged. "I'm beginning to see the appeal of this place. There's nothing here to cloud the mind or muddle the senses. It's all very...real."

She slowly approached. Her features came into focus and he could see her smiling. "We used to come out here on weekends. My brothers would ride out into the desert on dirt bikes and I'd tag along. I just assumed I was one of the boys."

"What happened?"

"I started growing up. Boys started noticing me. And my brothers told me I couldn't hang out with them anymore. That only made me more determined to do everything they did, only better."

"And what do you want now?"

"I just want to go back to my old life," she murmured. "I want things to be the way they were." She stood beside him. "I used to be able to take a guy like you down in a matter of seconds." Though it should have sounded like a threat, her words seemed more like foreplay to him.

"I'd like to see that," he murmured. The scent from her hair wafted on the breeze, and he took another breath, fighting the urge to bury his face in those silken strands.

"I just want my old life back again," she repeated softly.

"Your brother doesn't agree," Cameron said.

She looked over at him, her brow furrowed in confusion. "Tony? Has he been out here already? What did he tell you?"

"He told me I should leave you alone. And that if I hurt you, he'll take me out into the desert and—"

She pressed a finger to his lips. "Don't listen to him," Sofie said. "He has no idea what I need right now."

"He told me you had a guy. And that he broke your heart." Cameron reached down and smoothed his hand over her cheek, tipping her face up to his.

"No. He didn't break my heart. After the accident, I just couldn't give him what he needed. He was a detective in Major Crimes. Sam. We'd been dating for about a year. After the accident he just…hovered. He didn't know how to handle things. I think it shook him up. I was angry and sad and stubborn, up and down every day, just an emotional mess. And when I told him I wanted back on the force, he said that he couldn't support that. He didn't want to marry someone who'd always be in danger." She shrugged. "Nobody cares what I want."

"What do you want right now, Sofie? Tell me and I'll give it to you."

She pushed up on her toes and touched her lips

to his. Cameron sucked in a sharp breath then gathered her in his arms, pulling her against his body. A powerful desire coursed through him, pulsing with every beat of her heart. And as the kiss deepened, he smoothed his hands down to her backside.

This was crazy. He'd met her just that morning, and yet he was certain there wasn't any other woman in the world he wanted more. She was soft and sexy, and the way she responded to him was an invitation to take more.

But was he ready to do this, to take advantage of her vulnerability just to satisfy his needs? It was clear that she wanted him as much as he wanted her, but he couldn't help but wonder if they ought to wait.

As she wrapped her legs around his waist, her nightgown hiked up on her thighs. Cameron ran his palms along the smooth length of her legs then let his touch slide beneath her gown. To his shock, he realized she was naked beneath the soft cotton fabric.

He groaned inwardly, unable to stop himself from exploring further. Wild visions burst in his head as he imagined tugging the dress over her head to reveal her body. Had she planned this all along?

When he moved his hand up to her hip, she reached down and stopped him, pushing against his touch. Cameron didn't care about the scars or whatever she called imperfections. They were as much a part of Sofie as her silken hair and soft skin. He wanted to know every inch of her body intimately.

Cameron carried her toward the trailer, his mouth

still fixed on hers. The temptation was almost too much to resist, but he knew that they couldn't deny the inevitable. When they finally fell into bed together, it would be because they'd both thought through all the consequences and determined it was the only course of action left to them.

When they reached the door of the trailer, he gently unlocked her legs from around his waist and set her on her feet. His hands skimmed up her torso, brushing against the soft flesh of her breasts beneath the thin cotton. And when he reached her face, Cameron slowly drew back.

His heart was slamming in his chest, and his shaft, now hard and ready, pressed against the fabric of his faded jeans. "We have a long day tomorrow," he murmured.

Her fingers trailed over his naked chest, the sensation setting his nerves on fire. "Then we better get started," she said. As her hands drifted lower, to the waistband of his jeans, he caught her fingers, tangling them in his.

"Go to bed, Sofie. We both need a good night's sleep. I'll see you in the morning."

She opened her mouth to speak, but a soft gasp was all he heard. "But I thought we—"

"There's plenty of time for that," he assured her.

She stared up at him, her features washing with the harsh light filtering out of the trailer door. Her eyes closed and he kissed her again. "Good night, Sofie. I'll see you in the morning."

She nodded, then turned and walked toward the house, her hips swaying provocatively beneath the breeze-blown nightgown. Cameron swallowed hard, trying to convince himself that he'd done the right thing. Would there be a next time? Or would Sofie find a reason to push aside her desires and focus on the business at hand?

He opened the door of the trailer and stepped inside. It was a gamble he'd have to take. But the rewards would be worth the wait. When she finally crawled into his bed beside him, she'd be there for all the right reasons.

SOFIE STOOD OVER Cameron, her gaze taking in the details of his half-naked body. His right arm was thrown over his head, and one long leg hung off the edge of the small bed. She hadn't had much chance to study him without his awareness, but she took the opportunity now.

He was perhaps the most beautiful man she'd ever met. Though his body was finely muscled, he was lean and lithe, not enhanced by too many hours pumping iron in some gym. She liked that about him, that his body wasn't altered to fit some strange notion of masculine beauty. He was just a regular guy—but not that regular.

His dark hair was mussed, and long lashes rested on his suntanned cheeks. Her gaze drifted down to his mouth, and her mind spun back to the kisses they had shared the night before. Sofie had been attracted to him from the moment they met, but never in her life had she taken such liberties with a man after only knowing him for a day.

What had gotten into her? Why was it suddenly so simple to imagine sex with a complete stranger like Cameron when she'd avoided it for such a long time with other men who'd passed though her life?

Sofie knew what had happened with Sam had cut deep. The scars from the accident had destroyed her confidence with men. But sooner or later, she'd have to take a chance and allow herself a bit of romance in her life.

Even now, as she recalled the way Cameron had touched her and kissed her, she felt so alive, so hopeful. She hadn't experienced that kind of optimism in months. But she also knew the realities of this situation. Cameron didn't belong here and wouldn't be staying more than a month or two. Falling in love with him would be a ridiculous waste of time.

Sofie slowly sat down on the edge of the bed, setting the thermos of coffee on the floor beside her feet, taking care not to disturb him. She why couldn't she do like most men did—avoid the trap of mixing up sex and love?

She reached out to brush a strand of hair from his eyes, then stopped herself. Her hand trembled as she placed it on his bare chest. His skin was warm and smooth, and she could feel his heartbeat beneath her palm. Sofie shook him gently, but he didn't stir at first. Then, leaning close, she gently pressed her lips to his. When she drew back, his eyes were open and he was watching her.

"Morning," she murmured.

He smiled drowsily. "Morning? Is it morning?"

"Almost," she said. Sofie reached down for the thermos. "I brought you coffee."

He pushed up on his elbow. "I don't have to go to the Bunny Shack until lunch."

"I'm meeting a contact over at Millie's. He has to get to work so that's why we have to leave early. I brought you something."

"Coffee," he said with a smile.

"Something else." Sofie reached into her pocket and pulled out the fossil. It was one she'd found last month on one of her hikes into the desert. "Here. I thought you'd like this. I think it's part of a leg bone. Probably some kind of sauropod." She reached into her other pocket and pulled out a small field guide to fossils. "Here's a book."

"This is really a dinosaur bone?"

"Not a complete bone. Those are pretty rare. It's just a piece of one. But it will show you what to look for."

"We're going to dig for bones?"

"Not today. Walter usually spends the weekends in Albuquerque with his wife. My uncle takes over the case when he's there. But if you'd like, we can go this weekend, assuming Walter keeps to his usual routine. For now, it's time to get up." She stood and pulled the sheet off his body. Her gaze fell on the tented fabric of his boxers, and her breath caught in her throat. He was fully erect. The sheet slipped out of her hand. "Sorry."

He chuckled softly, glancing down at his lap. "Don't be. It happens. All the time."

Sofie cleared her throat. "Well, once you take care of that, get dressed. I'll be waiting for you outside."

Cameron sat up and swung his legs off the edge of the bed, ignoring the subject of their conversation. "Hand me that coffee," he said.

She opened the thermos and poured him a cup, the hot liquid steaming in the cool interior of the trailer. Suddenly, all she could think about was sex. An arousal like that really shouldn't go to waste. If she just reached out and touched him there, just a simple caress, the whole morning would change direction. It would be so simple.

He took a sip from the plastic cup and sighed softly. "Good," he said with a lazy smile. "So, who is this person we're going to meet?"

She blinked, her thoughts shifting again. "Jimmy Chaca. He's a bouncer at a roadhouse on the highway east of Holman. He also has a construction business and occasionally does work on Walter's ranch."

"Is he a snitch?"

"You need to stop watching *Law & Order*," she said. "He's a guy I know. He gets me information and I give him a little money. A snitch is a criminal who talks about other criminals. Jimmy is more like a confidential informant."

Cameron stretched his arms over his head and stood up, now unconcerned with the state of his arousal. Sofie couldn't help but steal another look. Why even bother to pretend that they weren't on the fast track to total surrender? It was just a matter of time. And courage.

He grabbed his jeans from the opposite sofa and stepped into them, leaving them unzipped for the moment while he brushed his teeth at the kitchen sink. When he found his T-shirt, Cameron pulled it over his head, wiping his mouth with the back of his hand.

"Shoes," she said, pointing to his bare feet.

He searched for a pair of socks and, after pulling them on, stepped into his new boots. Cameron stood in front of her, raking his hands through his hair. "All right, I'm ready."

Sofie shook her head and grabbed the thermos. "Put a shirt on. It's chilly. I've got a jacket for you in the Jeep." Then she pointed to his crotch. "Better zip up. You look like a pervert."

He laughed then picked up his new hat from the table and followed her out of the trailer, working at the zipper as he walked. The Jeep was waiting, and she hopped behind the wheel and started it up. Seconds later, they were tearing down the road, a plume of dust spreading out behind them.

Sofie wasn't sure where the day would lead, but she knew at the end of it, she and Cameron would be alone again, faced with the same choice they'd had last night. The morning air chilled her cheeks and she drew a deep breath. Perhaps tonight events would take an entirely different path.

"Are we going to get some breakfast at Millie's? I'm really hungry."

"We'll get you something for the road. I don't usually eat breakfast."

By they time they got to town, the sun was well above the horizon. Vulture Creek was quiet except for the crowd of pickup trucks parked in front of the diner. Millie's was always busy for breakfast. Sofie pulled up beside a battered red pickup and beeped her horn. A few minutes later, Jimmy stood next to the Jeep, his broad shoulders and raven hair instantly recognizable.

"Hey, Jimmy," Sofie said. "Jimmy Chaca, this is Cameron Quinn. He's going to be helping me out on this case. Cameron, this is Jimmy. What have you got?"

"There were some young kids in the bar last night from that dig over near the airstrip. They were talking about some meeting that their boss had a few days ago. Some older guy rolled into camp after midnight driving a blue Olds convertible. He left with a couple of wooden crates."

"Dinosaur bones?"

He shook his head. "Nope. Seems they're in charge of cataloging everything that comes out of the ground on that dig, and this wasn't something they'd seen before."

"Drugs," she murmured. Sofie raked her hand through her hair. "I was wondering how he was coming up with all this money. I thought he was taking political bribes."

"I also fixed a broken porch step over at the ranch and had a chance to go through Vivian's purse. Her name is Vivian Armstrong, and she has an Arizona driver's license and a Sedona address."

"Armstrong? You're sure?"

Jimmy nodded. "That's what it said."

She reached into her pocket and pulled out two twenties, then pressed them into his palm. "Thanks," she said. "Keep in touch."

"Will do." He glanced over at Cameron and nodded. "Watch her back."

"I will," Cameron said.

She watched as Jimmy walked away, then leaned back in her seat and closed her eyes. She drew a deep breath of the chilly morning air. "This is not good," she murmured.

"You think he's involved in drug smuggling?" Cameron asked.

"I don't know. But that's not the worst of it. Vivian Armstrong. Armstrong is the maiden name of Stella Fredericks, Walter's wife. I think he's sleeping with his sister-in-law."

"That's not good," Cameron said.

"This case just got way too complicated. How am I going to tell Stella about this?"

"Maybe your uncle should," Cameron suggested.

Sofie shook her head. "Oh, no. He'll leave it up to me. It's a woman thing. And my mother. She's going to be so upset."

"Why? What does your mother have to do with this?"

"Stella is one of her best friends. They've known each other for years. She helped my mother get her gallery started." Sofie cursed softly. "I hate when things get personal."

"I'm sorry," Cameron said.

"Why do men cheat? The world would be so much better if they just kept their pants on. But no, there's always something new and better around the next corner. Some sweet young thing with brand-new boobs and a tight ass."

"Not all men cheat," Cameron said.

"Maybe not. But they probably think about it." Sofie reached for the ignition. Where was a kiss when she really needed one? Right now, Sofie would enjoy any diversion from this uncomfortable turn of events. She glanced over at Cameron and weighed the consequences of indulging right there in the middle of Main Street.

"Sometimes, I really hate this job."

4

THE PARKING LOT OF the Bunny Shack began to fill shortly after noon. The place was located on the highway between Vulture Creek and Holman, a single building amid the desert landscape.

They'd put the canvas top up on the Jeep for shade, and Sofie sat slouched in the passenger seat, fiddling with her cell phone. Cameron glanced over at her. Since her discussion with Jimmy Chaca that morning, she'd been quiet and distracted, receiving and sending texts for most of the morning.

She was so lost in her thoughts that she didn't notice him watching. Cameron's mind wandered back to their early-morning encounter in the Airstream. How much longer would it be before they woke up together?

It was hard to ignore the desire he felt for her. But it wasn't just a physical attraction. He was curious about her, about the woman she was. He wanted to know everything about her—what made her laugh,

what made her cry, what made her sigh with pleasure. But they'd been so busy with the case, they'd
barely had time to talk about anything else.

After meeting Jimmy Chaca, they'd driven out to
the airstrip to look around. She returned to Millie's
to ask the woman about the people from the dig and
any suspicious behavior that might have been noted.
Then they'd driven into Harmon to use the library
Wi-Fi to do a search on the head of the dinosaur dig,
Dr. Leonard Crowley.

"Are you going to tell me what's going on?" Cameron asked.

She looked up. "What?"

"What's with all the texts? Does it have something
to do with the case? I'm your assistant investigator—
I think you need to keep me informed."

She blinked. "I've been talking with my brother
Marco. The one in the DEA. I was asking him if
anything had popped up on their radar with the dig
near the airstrip."

"And what did he say?"

"No," Sofie replied. "Nothing." She frowned. "I
can see how it might work. With the airstrip about
two miles away, they could fly the drugs in at night,
move them over to the dig on ATVs and then just
ship them out with whatever dinosaur bones they've
found."

"But what does Walter have to do with any of
this?"

"That's what I don't get," Sofie said. She twisted

in her seat to face him. "If he's involved in drug running, then this case is much more complicated than I thought. Maybe he found out about the operation and is shaking them down? Cheating on his wife is one thing, but there's a whole other level of violence that comes along with drugs."

"I can imagine," Cameron said.

"No, you can't. You have no idea how far these guys are willing to go to protect their territory. They wouldn't think twice before shooting anyone who might get in their way." She shook her head. "Maybe this isn't such a good idea after all."

"I'm just going to go inside, sit down, have a little lunch and chat with a few of the patrons."

"But don't move too quickly." Sofie handed him her cell phone. "If you can't remember details, just excuse yourself to make a phone call and record them. Just push that button on the side. It's all set up. And if an opening doesn't present itself, then don't force it. I don't want you to—"

Cameron reached out and pressed his finger to her lips. "It's no big deal. Don't worry."

She nodded, then pressed a wad of bills into his palm. "Tip the girls. Buy yourself some lunch. There's enough there for one lap dance but I'd appreciate it if you didn't enjoy it."

Cameron looked down at the money and grinned. "I can hardly wait to tell my brothers about this," he said. "They're probably out there working some boring job for minimum wage, and I'm having lunch at the Bunny Shack."

"Don't get too excited," she said.

"I'm sure I can control myself," Cameron said.

Just then, Sofie straightened in her seat, her gaze fixed on the side-view mirror. "There he is. Blue Olds convertible."

Cameron watched as Walter Fredericks parked his car in the first row, about ten yards from the front door. Though Cameron had studied the photo in Sofie's file, the man who climbed out of the car was much smaller than he'd imagined. He was also older, his hair now completely gray instead of the salt-and-pepper of the photo.

"Just don't be too eager. Just play it cool at first and—"

This time he decided to stop her advice with a kiss. He grabbed her face between his hands and pressed his lips to hers. Slowly, he softened the kiss until her lips parted beneath his. They'd become so familiar with each other that kissing was easy, almost instinctual. There was no hesitation, no clumsiness, only a simple expression of need.

But he knew it wouldn't be long before the desire overwhelmed them. With Sofie's mercurial nature, it might happen in an hour or sometime next month.

Strangely, that didn't bother him. He knew it would be worth waiting for. He drew back and looked into her eyes. "This is so strange. I'm kissing you in the parking lot, and I'm about to go stuff dollar bills into other women's G-strings."

Sofie groaned, pushing him back. "Just act like you're having fun."

He nodded, then opened the door and stepped out of the Jeep. He glanced back once before walking inside, but he couldn't see her through the sun's reflection.

The Bunny Shack wasn't quite what Cameron expected. The interior was shabby and worn and smelled of stale beer and cigarette smoke. The music blared out of speakers that were tinny and distorted. And the women, though not unattractive, plied their trade with a casual boredom that didn't add much to the experience.

He scanned the room, a maze of elevated runways with bar stools lining the edges. Cameron settled in a few seats away from Walter Fredericks, then ordered a beer from a scantily clad waitress.

He wasn't quite sure where to look. Everywhere he turned there was naked flesh, but it wasn't the naked flesh he wanted to see. It was difficult for him to believe that any man found this atmosphere sexually arousing. He was more turned on by the scent of Sofie's hair than the sight of a half-clad female writhing in front of him.

Cameron observed the dancers distractedly as he sipped his beer, his mind wandering to the woman waiting for him out in the parking lot. His mind substituted an image of Sofie, dressed in lingerie, her lithe body moving in front of him.

He watched out of the corner of his eye as another waitress delivered lunch to Fredericks and the older man took a huge bite of a burger. Food. The perfect conversation starter.

"How's the food here?" Cameron asked. "Any good?"

Walter wiped his mouth with a paper napkin and nodded, still chewing. "It's not bad," he said, nodding. "Stick with the burgers and sandwiches. Everything else is pretty bland."

"Thanks," Cameron said. He took a sip of his beer. "Can't go wrong with a cold beer and a little entertainment."

"Nope, I'd have to agree with that," Walter said.

"So, do you live here in town?" Cameron asked.

"Yeah, I've got a place nearby. But I spend most of my time in Albuquerque. Where are you from?"

Cameron slowly turned on his stool, bracing his arm on the edge of the bar. "Seattle. But I'm thinking of settling around here. I'm tired of the rain. You've got plenty of sun around here."

"We do have that in abundance. So, are you looking to buy or rent a place?"

"I'm not really worried about buying somewhere to live right now. I'm just looking for some good investment opportunities."

Walter stood up and moved over another seat, sliding his plate along the bar. "Well, now, you picked the right place. And I just happen to be a real-estate broker. I could show you some things."

"I'm not just interested in real estate," Cameron said. "I'm looking for anything that can make me some fast cash, if you know what I mean."

"So, you're willing to take some risk for a big reward?"

"Yeah, that's exactly what I'm looking to do," Cameron said.

For the next fifteen minutes, Walter regaled him with stories of his own investment schemes, ranging from golf courses to oil wells. Unfortunately, nothing the man mentioned came close to being illegal. Cameron decided to play hard to get, hoping that Walter might tempt him with something more interesting, but the older man obviously still had a few suspicions.

"You mentioned you were from Seattle. What do you do up there?"

"I design custom sailing yachts," Cameron said.

That brought a look of surprise and Walter laughed. "If you're looking for waterfront property, you won't find it around here."

Cameron laughed, then glanced down at his watch. "Oh, hell. I've got to go. I have an appointment with an agent here in town and—"

"Cancel it," Walter said. "You're not going to find anyone better than me. I'm plugged in. I know everyone in town." He reached into his shirt pocket and pulled out a business card, then slid it along the bar to Cameron. "Give me a few days to set up some things. I'll let you in on a deal or two that no one else has access to. Monday morning would be—"

"I'm really interested in looking this weekend," Cameron said with a shrug.

Walter sat back and sighed. "Hey, I wish I could, but I've got plans." He lowered his voice. "Truth is, my girlfriend is taking me to a spa in Taos for our anniversary. What the hell am I going to do at a spa?"

Cameron took a swig of his beer. "Hell if I know."

"Well, you know how the ladies love their pampering. You married?"

Cameron shook his head. "I just like to look, not buy."

"Smart man. You make all your own decisions. You don't have to check with the little woman before you invest."

"Well, Mr. Fredericks. Why don't we plan on meeting here for lunch on Monday?" Cameron suggested. "And then we'll get some business done."

Walter held out his hand. "I don't even know your name."

"Cameron Quinn." He finished the last of his beer then tossed a ten-dollar tip down next to the empty bottle. "I'll be in touch," he said as he pushed up from his stool.

He was almost to the door when Walter approached him from behind. "Hey, listen. I'm going to be at the Serenity Spa and Resort in Taos. What do you say I get you a room there for Saturday night—

my treat—and we can find some time to talk busi-ness? You just enjoy yourself, have a seaweed wrap or a massage, play a round of golf, and then we can get together for drinks. You can even meet my Viv-ian. You'll like her."

"I don't know," Cameron said. "I'm really not much of a spa guy."

"Most guys aren't. But there'll be plenty of good-looking women there, without their husbands, if you know what I mean. A guy like you is bound to get lucky."

"I'll think about it," Cameron said.

"You do that!" Walter called.

Cameron strolled to the front doors and out into the afternoon sun, squinting against the light. Sofie was waiting in the far corner of the parking lot, sit-ting in the passenger seat of the Jeep, her eyes closed, the wires from her iPod dangling from her ears.

He slipped in behind the wheel. Startled, she sat up. "You're back already?"

He turned the ignition and threw the Jeep into Re-verse. "He invited me to the Serenity Spa in Taos. He and Vivian are leaving tonight. He said I should join them tomorrow night."

"What? Join them? Like in—a threesome?"

"I don't think so," Cameron said, frowning. "Jeez, I hope that's not what he meant. I just think he wants to throw some money around and impress me. He and Vivian are spending their anniversary there. And he doesn't want to wait until Monday to talk business." Cameron groaned. "He said I'd really like Vivian. Did that mean he planned to...share her?"

"Just drive," Sofie said, pointing to the road. "I need some time to figure this all out."

Sofie sat at the small table inside the Airstream, picking at the remains of the take-out dinner they'd picked up from Millie's. After Cameron's visit to the Bunny Shack, they'd visited the county courthouse in Gallup to check on the deed to the ranch where Vivian was living.

To Sofie's surprise, Vivian Armstrong was listed as the sole owner on the deed. Sofie knew that Vivian and Stella had money from their father's estate, but why would a single woman choose to live out in the middle of nowhere? Vulture Creek was at least an hour outside of Albuquerque. Certainly she and Walter didn't need that much distance to keep their affair a secret.

Sofie had never really understood the kind of woman who'd cede control of her life to a man. Even with Sam, she had made all her own decisions. Maybe that was why it hadn't worked out. But it was hard to trust someone with her life, and her heart.

She glanced across the table at Cameron and smiled. They'd known each other for two days, and yet she sensed he was the trustworthy type, in every sense.

"You're awfully quiet," Cameron said.

She glanced up at him and smiled. "You did a good job today. I couldn't have done what you did."

"It was kind of fun. Pretending. It was a new challenge."

"Sometimes I wonder if that might be what I need. A challenge."

Cameron reached out and took her hand, weaving his fingers through hers. "Like what?"

"I don't know. That's the problem. So much of my life has been tied up with being a cop." Sofie shook her head, then pushed to her feet. "I should do these dishes. Are you done eating?"

"Sofie, we can talk about this. I'm a good listener."

"No, it's just something I have to figure out on my own." She picked up his plate and hers and carried them to the small sink.

"I really enjoyed today," Cameron said.

"Even the naked girls?" she asked.

"No. I mean, they were friendly and they knew how to dance pretty well, for strippers that is. But I liked trying something new. For about fifteen minutes I felt like a private investigator." He stood and finished clearing the table. "It's strange," Cameron continued. "When we were driving back here, I was thinking about what my grandfather had said, about trying out a different life. And I got to wondering what things would have been like if my parents hadn't disappeared on that trip."

Just the thought of what he'd gone through as a

boy was enough to bring tears to her eyes. She saw the aftereffects in the man he'd become—so careful and controlled. At times, he could be funny and relaxed, and then, in the blink of an eye, he'd lose himself in his thoughts.

"It must have been hard."

"I don't think much about it."

She turned the tap and filled the sink with warm water.

"Let me do that," Cameron said. "I'm supposed to be earning my keep here."

Sofie handed him a dish towel. "You can dry," she said.

He took the towel from her hand, then grabbed her waist and pulled her away from the sink. "I think we can leave those for later. Let's take a walk. I need some fresh air."

The sun was nearly at the horizon, the western sky blazing in colors of orange and pink and purple. Cameron took her hand and they walked out behind the trailer. The desolation of the high desert was spread out in front of them, and they walked toward the sunset, the landscape bathed in a pink hue.

"It's a lot like the ocean," Cameron murmured after he drew a deep breath. "Just a big expanse of nothingness. It makes everyday details seem kind of small and insignificant."

"When we were kids, my grandfather used to take us out into the desert. He'd teach us all survival skills and talk to us about the Hopi culture, what it meant to live in the world and not on it."

"John Muir," Cameron said.

She nodded. "My grandfather was a big fan. We used to study everything and discuss its purpose in the desert. 'When we try to pick out anything by itself,'" she quoted, "'we find it hitched to everything else in the Universe.' That's how the desert works."

"I like that," Cameron said.

"I learned to make fire without matches and how to find water. The ultimate test for my brothers was to spend forty-eight hours alone in the desert."

"Really?" Cameron asked.

Sofie nodded. "All of them had done it by the time they turned thirteen. My grandfather said it was a rite of passage, the time when boys became men. But when it was my turn, they wouldn't let me go. I begged and begged, but my parents told me that I couldn't."

"I suspect that was the wrong thing to say to you," Cameron said, smiling down at her.

"I was so mad. I told myself that when I grew up, I would never, ever let anyone make decisions for me." She kicked at a small rock with the toe of her boot. "Sometimes, I think that was the moment I decided that I would show them all that they were wrong about me." She shrugged. "Maybe I should have learned to be more flexible."

"No," Cameron said. "You're strong and independent. You know what you want. You don't need to change, Sofie." He pulled her into his embrace. "I like you just the way you are."

He stared down at her, his gaze searching hers. When his lips touched hers, Sofie clutched at his shirt, her body feeling suddenly boneless. "You're not scared of anything, are you?" Cameron said.

Sofie's first response was the one she always had when challenged by her brothers. No, she wasn't scared of anything. But if she really thought about it, there were a lot of things that scared her. As she looked up at Cameron, she realized that maybe she didn't always have to be the toughest woman in the room. "That's not true," she said.

"What are you afraid of?"

"I'm afraid my hip will never get better. I'm afraid I'll never get to be a cop again. I'm afraid I'll—" She stopped, realizing that she'd already said too much.

"What? Say it."

"I'm afraid I might always be alone. There. I said the thing that every woman shouldn't say. The reason that women stay in horrible relationships."

"No," he said, hugging her tight. "You won't be alone."

Sofie pulled out of his embrace and strode toward the sunset. It didn't help to have him here, touching her and kissing her whenever she needed reassurance. She'd already come to crave those moments when she forgot who she was and just…reacted.

She heard his footsteps behind her and then felt the touch of his hand on her shoulder. "Did you ever do that quest, you know, spend the two nights in the desert? All on your own?"

Sofie sighed. "I did. I was fourteen and we were here visiting my uncle. I grabbed a sleeping bag and some supplies and just walked out there," she said, pointing. "I didn't tell anyone where I was going."

"And?"

"I was terrified. I didn't sleep at all the first night. By the second night, I was so exhausted, I slept like the dead. And when I got home, I was grounded for six months." She paused. "I feel that same kind of fear right now."

"Are you afraid of me?"

"No. Well, yes, kind of. I'm afraid that you'll…"

"What?" Cameron asked, turning her chin up until their eyes met.

"I—I'm afraid you'll change me. You'll…knock me off course. I know what I want, Cameron. And a guy like you doesn't really fit into those plans, no matter how much fun it is to kiss you and touch you."

He forced a smile, fixing his gaze somewhere over her shoulder. "I'm not sure what to say to that. Sofie, I don't want to make you do anything you don't want to."

A tiny laugh escaped her lips. "Yeah, well, you may not mean to do it, but you do anyway."

Cameron reached up and ran the back of his hand over her cheek, then furrowed his fingers through her hair. She knew he wanted to kiss her and could see what it was costing him to resist. But this had already gone too far. They'd known each other two days, and she was a heartbeat away from falling into bed with him.

"So what's our next move?" Cameron asked.

"We're going to go to Taos tomorrow, and you're going to meet with Walter. I'm going to get a room for myself, then hang around and see if I can catch a photo of him with Vivian. He's never seen me, so I think I'll be safe. And then—"

"I meant about us," Cameron interrupted. "Where do you and I go from here?"

Sofie drew a deep breath. "I'm your boss and you're my employee."

She could see her answer wasn't what he wanted to hear. And it was the last thing she wanted to say. But this was already getting too dangerous, and she was ill-prepared to handle an affair with him. It would be best to stop while they still could.

"You know, maybe I should do a quest of my own." He turned and started toward the Airstream. "That's what I'm going to do. I'm going to grab a sleeping bag and some supplies and just walk out into the desert."

"You can't do that," Sofie said. "You have no idea what's out there. You'll get lost. You'll get bitten by a snake or a spider, and then I'll have to go find you and drag you back here."

He spun around, stopping her in her tracks. "Then come with me," he said. "Let's do it. We don't have to leave until late tomorrow morning."

"I can't," she said. "We shouldn't."

"Which is it, Sofie?"

"Both," she said.

"Well, if you want to play it safe, that's fine. But as long as I'm here, I'm going see what I'm made of."

Sofie cursed as she hurried after him. This was the last thing she needed. They should be focusing on the case, discussing strategies for tomorrow, going over the possible scenarios. "Can't you see what you're made of some other night?"

"I think a night alone in the desert is exactly what I need right now," Cameron said.

HE DIDN'T NEED TO walk far to lose sight of the ranch house. Cameron had navigated the open ocean without sight of land, steering by the stars. He wasn't afraid he'd get lost as Sofie had predicted. He'd picked out a point on the horizon and walked until the sun was nearly gone.

He found a spot in the shelter of a rocky outcropping. A nearby wash had enough wood to start a small fire, and he gathered it by the last light of the day. Unfortunately, the lighter he'd grabbed from the Airstream was out of fluid, so he was left with nothing but a pile of wood.

Cameron sat down and stared up at the first star in the deep blue sky. The silence all around him was almost deafening. It was so quiet he could hear himself thinking.

What the hell was doing here? He ought to be back

in Seattle, perfecting the new hull design he'd been working on. But in two days, he'd managed to forget all about that life and just slipped into this one. He cursed softly. If his real life was so forgettable, what did that say about it?

Part of it was the girl, he mused. She was the most intriguing woman he'd ever met. But his infatuation for her was bound to fade, as it had with every other woman in his life.

Too bad he couldn't make it disappear just by sheer will. Then they'd both be happy. But there was no denying how he felt when he touched her. It took all his willpower to keep himself from stripping them both naked and indulging in the desire that they both tried so hard to control.

He understood her fears. He'd had the same fears himself. For as long as he could remember, he'd avoided commitment, afraid that once he found someone to love he was bound to lose her, just like he lost his parents. If fate could destroy his family in the blink of an eye, then it could certainly destroy any relationship he cherished just as quickly.

But maybe those fears had affected him more than he'd realized. He'd always made the safe decision, the conservative choice. When it came time to choose a career, he didn't even consider stepping outside the comfort of the family business.

And yet now, with his world upside down, Cameron realized that he really hadn't been living his life. He'd just been…going along. And worse than that, he wasn't really happy.

"Nice fire."

The sound of her voice came out of nowhere, causing him to jump to his feet. An instant later, she shined a flashlight in his eyes. "Jaysus, you scared me."

"Lucky I wasn't a pack of coyotes looking for a late-night snack." Sofie slipped her backpack off her shoulders and set it down on the dry ground, then bent over the pile of firewood. A few seconds later, the kindling flickered, then caught.

"Thanks," Cameron said. "How did you find me?"

"My grandfather taught us to track. You're not hard to follow. You have very big feet." She poked at the fire with a stick.

"Why did you come?"

"I would never forgive myself if something happened to you out here. I wasn't going to get any sleep tonight worrying about you. So, I figured if I was out here with you we'd both have a chance to sleep." She turned and began to rummage through her pack. "Tent," Sofie said.

"Real men don't sleep in tents," he teased.

"Well, I do. You can sleep out here if you want, but I'm going inside. Stay close to the fire. It'll ward off the snakes and spiders and—"

"Lions and tigers?"

Sofie laughed. "A few bears, too." She untied the drawstring on the tent bag and dumped the contents on the ground. "There's a lantern in my pack. Why don't you pull that out and light it up?"

Cameron bent over her backpack and began to remove the contents. He pulled out a package of marshmallows and two campfire forks, then held them out to her. "What's this?"

"Dessert," she said.

"I thought I was supposed to be roughing it."

"You're a city boy."

"I have been camping before. Besides, I came out here to see if I was tough enough."

She grabbed the marshmallows and put them back in her pack. "All right. You don't get any s'mores, then. And since you're tough, you can finish setting up the tent."

Luckily the tent was similar to the one his brother Ronan owned, so he managed to get it up and staked in about fifteen minutes. He laid their sleeping bags inside, then joined her by the campfire.

She stared into the flames as she roasted a pair of marshmallows, slowly turning them. When they were finished, she held the fork out to him. "You first," she murmured.

He popped the nearly melted marshmallow into his mouth. "Mmm. Good." Cameron watched her for a long moment as she picked at hers. "So why did you really come out here? I'm pretty sure I would have survived the night."

"I feel responsible for you," Sofie said. "You're my employee."

"Is that all there is to it?" Cameron asked. He wanted her to tell him that there was much more, that she'd changed her mind about this attraction between them, that she didn't want to deny herself. "You can admit it, Sofie." He leaned closer, drawing in a deep breath, the scent of her shampoo sweet on the night air.

Sofie sighed softly. "It's not that I don't want to be with you. I feel it, too. Every time you touch me or kiss me, I can imagine how it would be. But we've only just met. And when it comes to men, I just don't trust myself."

"I don't understand."

"You're a nice guy. More than nice. You're the kind of man my mother wants me to marry. And it would be so easy for me to just surrender to that, to take the easy way out."

"You think love and marriage are easy?"

Sofie got to her feet and brushed off her hands on the front of her jeans. "I'm going to go back. Now that you have the tent and a fire, you'll be good on your own."

Cameron grabbed her hand. "Don't. Sofie, I understand. I'm not going to force the issue."

She nodded. "I know. But I might."

Cameron watched silently as she grabbed the flashlight and turned it on. "You sure you can find your way back?" he asked.

"Sure. I know this desert like the back of my hand. And see that brightness over there? That's the yard light at the ranch. Just in case you need to find your way back in the dark. I'll leave it on." She drew a ragged breath. "I'll see you tomorrow morning, Cameron."

He watched her disappear into the darkness, her footsteps echoing in the silent night air. Of all the women he'd ever known, there wasn't one who was smart enough or brave enough to walk through the desert in the middle of the night.

The fire popped and he grabbed one of the forks, loading it with marshmallows. He glanced over at the tent, visible in the light from the fire. She was right to go back, he thought to himself. There was no way they'd spend the night in that tent and not give in to what they both wanted.

In the distance, a coyote howled and Cameron smiled to himself. "How-ooooo," he sang, the sound carrying off into the distance. He listened and thought he heard a laugh from somewhere in the dark.

His thoughts wandered to his brothers. Where were they and what were they doing? Had they settled into a job, a place to live? In six weeks, they'd be together again. What kind of stories would they have to tell?

5

THEY CHECKED INTO the Serenity Spa and Resort separately, Cameron going in first and Sofie following a half hour later. She signed the register as Sofie Smith from San Francisco, following the story she and Cameron had decided on earlier. She was at the spa recovering after a skiing accident that injured her right leg.

The drive to Taos had been pleasant, but neither one of them had restarted the conversation they'd had the night before. For now, Cameron was doing his best to behave like a proper employee.

Sofie glanced up and down the hallway before knocking on the door of room 327. A moment later the door swung open and she hurried inside. Cameron stood behind her as she entered the room and took in her surroundings.

A king-size bed dominated his room. Near the French doors to the veranda, a sofa and coffee table provided a place to lounge. She walked over to the doors and gazed down at the turquoise water of the swimming pool. "I have a view of the parking lot," she complained.

If she hadn't been here to close a case, then this might have been the perfect place for a getaway with a sexy companion. In truth, Sofie had spent most of last night reconsidering her decision to keep her relationship with Cameron purely professional.

Maybe it was time to start living her life a bit more spontaneously. She always had a plan, a goal and a way to reach it. But where had that gotten her? After nearly dying, she ought to be the first person to want to live each day as if it were her last.

"What's your room number?" Cameron asked.

"I'm in 308. A few doors down from the elevator."

A twelve-year-old bottle of scotch sat on the table along with a card. She picked it up, read it, then turned back to Cameron. "A massage with Erika? Compliments of your new buddy, Walter. How nice of him."

"I can always cancel," he said.

"When are you supposed to meet him?"

"He left a message that we'll get together for a drink later this evening at the bar. He said he'd call."

Sofie sat down on the edge of the bed. The decor in Cameron's room was simple and serene, with touches of luxury throughout. Two plush robes hung from hooks on the wall, and the bedclothes were made of expensive cotton. She'd caught a glimpse of the bathroom on her way in and had noticed a walk-in shower big enough for two.

"Do you want a drink? There is a minibar." Cameron crossed to the small fridge and opened it. He bent down to pick through the contents. "No alcohol. I guess that's why he left the scotch."

"I'll have scotch," she said, suddenly feeling an attack of nerves.

If this was what she really wanted, then she shouldn't be nervous at all, Sofie mused. She ought to be calm and prepared. After all, she had always been cool in a crisis. And this certainly could be considered a dangerous situation.

Cameron dropped ice cubes into a pair of glasses, the sound shattering the silence, then poured a bit of scotch into each. He crossed the room, handed a glass to Sofie and sat down beside her. "Cheers," he said, clinking his glass against hers.

"Cheers," she murmured before taking a sip. The scotch burned a path down her throat and she stifled a cough.

"I got the impression we'd be meeting before dinner. Maybe five or six."

Sofie nodded. "I got a text from Walter's wife. She thinks he's at a conference in San Diego. She was thinking of surprising him there with a little visit."

"What did you tell her?"

"I told her to leave the investigation to me."

He took a sip of his scotch. "It seems like a waste not to enjoy ourselves while we're here."

"I don't think we should be seen together," Sofie said.

"Why not? We could pretend that we met at the pool and hit it off. You're Sofie Smith from San Francisco, and you're into healthy eating, yoga and good books. I saw you across the crowd and told myself I just had to meet you."

"I suppose that could work. It does seem like a waste of a perfectly good weekend."

"Maybe I could even bring you along for drinks. Then you could meet the cheating couple."

"I need to get photos," Sofie said. "That's going to be hard to do if I'm sitting at the table. I forgot my lipstick camera."

"You have one of those?" he asked.

Sofie laughed. "No. But I do have a digital recorder that looks like a pen." She considered her options for a long moment. "You go meet them first and I'll join you later. I'll walk by your table, and we can pretend it's just a chance meeting. Then you can invite me to join you."

He took another sip of his scotch. "All right. That sounds like a plan. So, what do we do until he calls?"

"Wait?" she said.

Cameron nodded.

"Or—or I guess we could order something to eat? Or maybe take a walk. We could go sit by the pool and—"

Her words were interrupted by his touch. Cameron reached out and ran his fingers along her jaw, then dragged his thumb over her lower lip. Her breath caught in her throat and she closed her eyes. She wanted to tell him to stop, but she didn't have the strength.

"And maybe I could kiss you," he added. He gaze fixed on hers and he waited.

She reminded herself to breathe, and then, without thinking of all the consequences, Sofie nodded. "Yes," she murmured. "Yes."

THEY FELL BACK onto the bed, and Cameron wrapped his arms around her, pulling her body into his. She couldn't think of a single reason to stop him. To Sofie's surprise, she wasn't afraid. This was what was meant to happen.

The kiss grew more intense, more desperate, and as Cameron ran his hands over her body, Sofie felt as if she was on sensory overload. His taste, his scent, the feel of his body beneath her hands was more than she could process, and she willed herself to slow down and enjoy each moment.

When he rolled over on top of her, she wriggled beneath him, their bodies creating a delicious friction that made her pulse pound. The evidence of his need was growing harder, and Sofie arched against him, determined to make her own need obvious.

If Cameron thought she still had doubts, he didn't make any move to stop. He pinned her hands above her head and dropped a trail of kisses along her neck and collarbone. "Tell me we don't have to stop," he whispered.

"No, we don't have to stop."

He drew her down into another kiss, this time lingering over her lips and teasing at her tongue until they were both sure of where they were headed. When he pulled her on top of him, Sofie sat up, her legs straddling his hips. She reached for the hem of her T-shirt and pulled it over her head.

Cameron's gaze flickered at the sight of her red satin bra, and he reached out and ran his fingers along the lacy strap. Sofie closed her eyes as he slipped his fingers beneath the strap and dragged it over her shoulder. Taking her cue, Sofie brushed aside the other strap, then reached back and unhooked the bra, letting it fall onto his chest.

He stared at her for a long moment, his gaze drifting down to her breasts. Sofie took a steadying breath. Everything in her life seemed to fade into the background. This was a moment she didn't want to forget. What stroke of good fortune had put him in her path? His grandfather could have bought him a ticket for another town, in another state, and he might never have met her.

Though Sofie had never believed in fate, she was forced to think that there was something beyond luck that had brought them together. Karma? Kismet? Would something like this happen without any reason?

"You're the most beautiful thing I've ever seen," he said.

A smile twitched at the corners of her mouth. "If you say that again, I might believe you."

He cupped the warm flesh of her breast in his hand, teasing her nipple until it came to a hard peak. "You are…the most beautiful—"

She didn't let him finish. She bent down and stopped his words with her lips. In that single moment, Sofie knew that they wouldn't be able to stop. They'd take this seduction to its logical conclusion, and after that, their relationship would be irrevocably changed.

He sat up, pulling her closer, then tugged his own T-shirt over his head. Sofie wrapped her arms around him and drew him to her body, his lips pressed against her chest. Slowly, he moved lower until he found her nipple. Cameron flicked his tongue around the hard peak, causing a low moan to tear from Sofie's throat.

Holding tight to her waist, he crawled back to the center of the bed, and she stretched out beside him. They paused, staring into each other's eyes, waiting for the other to call a halt to the seduction.

"It's been a long time since I've done this," she whispered.

"Me, too," he replied.

Sofie shook her head. "No, I mean a really long… long time. Since before my accident. I'm not sure I'm going to—"

"Don't worry," he said. "We'll go very slowly."

She reached for the button of his jeans and undid it. "I think I want this." Slowly, she drew the zipper down. "And this."

He reached over to her jeans. "Do you want this?" Cameron asked, his hands on the button.

Sofie nodded. She wanted it all. The undeniable need, the shivers of pleasure, the weight of his body as he rolled on top of her. Her body ached for his touch, every nerve so alive that Sofie wondered whether she'd ever find relief.

He crawled off the bed and pulled her to her feet, slowly skimming her jeans over her hips. "Boots first," Sofie said, sitting down on the edge of the bed.

Cameron tugged them off, then kicked off his own. Jeans and socks came next, and when Cameron was left with just his boxers and Sofie her red panties, they stopped again for a moment.

She wasn't sure how they'd gotten to this point and she really didn't care. They'd been teetering on the edge since the moment he'd first touched her, pretending that there was nothing between them. But they couldn't avoid it any longer.

She reached out for the waistband of his boxers, but a knock sounded on the door and Sofie froze. "Do you think that's him?" she asked.

"Who is it?" Cameron called.

"It's Erika. I'm here for your massage. I was told to come by at three. I'm set up down at the pool if you'd like to come down."

He grabbed a robe and pulled it on, then walked to the door. Sofie stepped out of view and listened as he spoke softly to the masseuse.

"I'm kind of busy right now," he said. "Maybe I could reschedule for another time. I'm really sorry but—"

"No problem," Erika said. "Just dial eight-seven. Have a nice evening, Mr. Quinn."

Sofie heard the door close and smiled. She stepped out of the shadows. "Put out the sign, Mr. Quinn," she said. "We don't want to be disturbed again."

CAMERON FELT HER arms around his waist as he shut the door. He closed his eyes and smiled. Though he'd expected that they'd maintain their distance as she promised last night, Cameron had decided that he wasn't going to encourage that point of view. Still, he hadn't expected things to move quite so quickly.

He grabbed her hands and brought them to his lips, pressing a kiss into each palm. She nuzzled the center of his back, and Cameron turned and grabbed her waist, pulling her against him. "I don't know, that massage sounded really good. Maybe I should call Erika back," he teased.

"Don't you dare. I'm not sure I could stand the competition."

Cameron reached down and picked her up, carrying Sofie to the bed. He dropped her onto the mattress, then fell down beside her. "She's no competition," he said. "She had a wart on her nose and was missing her front tooth."

"I have a limp," Sofie said.

"I don't even notice that," he said. Cameron braced himself on his elbow, then ran his hand along her right hip. The scar was there, partially hidden by the high waist of her satin panties. He pulled the fabric away and looked at it, tracing the jagged shape of it with his finger.

"It's ugly," she said.

He shook his head. "No. It's part of you. It's beautiful." Cameron leaned over and pressed a kiss to her hip. "Everyone has scars. I have this one myself." He pointed to his hairline. "I got whacked in the head with a boom. Knocked me right off the boat. I almost drowned."

"What's a boom? Like a boom box?"

"No, it's the horizontal support for a mainsail." He held up his hand in the shape of an L. "See, the sail is attached along the mast, and the boom moves it from one side to the other so it can catch the wind. Sixteen stitches and it bled like crazy." He paused. "I know it's small potatoes next to your scar, but it hurt."

She laughed. "Small potatoes?"

"Yes. Small potatoes." Cameron put on his best Irish accent. "My grandda always says that. 'Och, boyo, don't worry about it. It's small potatuhs.'"

Sofie reached up and ran her hand through his hair and smiled. She had the most incredible smile and when she turned it toward him, Cameron felt the warmth of it like the sun on his face.

"It's hard to believe we only met a few days ago," she said.

"Considering where we are and what we're doing, I'd have to agree with you there," Cameron said.

"I don't want to wait any longer," Sofie said.

"There is something to be said for anticipation, though." He brushed her lips with his. "Maybe we could just lie here and get to know each other a bit better. You could ask me a question. I could ask you a question. I could show you more of my scars."

"Or maybe we could just take off the rest of our clothes and see what develops," Sofie suggested.

"I suppose I could always be persuaded," he said.

Sofie reached between them and ran her hand over the front of his boxers. Cameron groaned softly, then grabbed her wrist. "Don't start something you aren't planning to finish," he warned.

"I'm prepared to finish," she said.

Cameron nearly jumped out of his skin when she slipped her hand beneath the waistband and wrapped her fingers around his hard shaft. Her touch sent a surge of pleasure racing through his body.

Somewhere in their lazy exploration, they managed to discard Cameron's boxers and her red satin panties. He left her alone on the bed for a moment to retrieve condoms from his shaving kit, and when he returned, she took the two packets from his outstretched fingers.

"Were you planning for this?" she asked. "Or do you always carry protection?"

"I never planned for this," he said. "And I do usually carry protection."

Cameron skimmed his hand from her hip to her belly and then dipped lower to touch the spot between her legs. Her body seemed to melt into his, and he knew his caress had the intended effect. Her eyes closed; her lips parted slightly.

As he brought her closer to her release, she reached around him, her fingers closing around his erection. Slowly, she stroked him, bringing Cameron along with her.

It was so simple, each of them teasing the other, testing the limits of their control, searching for the one caress that would bring the ultimate experience. Cam sensed that she was near, and knew exactly what it would take to send her over the edge.

But when she cried out, then dissolved into a series of deep spasms, he wasn't prepared for the effect that it would have on him. In a heartbeat, Cam was there with her, unbearably tense and then incredibly relaxed. He tried to stop himself, but the sound of her pleasure was enough to send him over the edge.

When it was finally over, when the last of their tremors had dissolved, she nuzzled against his chest. Sofie drew a ragged breath. "Oops," she whispered.

He chuckled, pulling her close to kiss the top of her head. "Oops," he replied. "We'll have to try that again. Best to get it right."

"You know what I'd like to try? I'd like to take a long shower and then wrap myself up in that robe over there and order room service. I'm starving."

"Then go," he said. "I hope you don't mind if I watch?"

She crawled off the bed and stood beside it, her dark hair tumbling over her shoulders. He'd tried to imagine the body beneath the faded jeans and simple shirts, but Cameron had never pictured anything like this. From top to toe, she was sheer perfection—long legs and slender hips, a tiny waist and small breasts.

"Are you done looking now?" she asked.

"Not quite. Turn around."

With a laugh, she spun on her heel and walked over to the rack with the robes. A moment later, she'd wrapped her body in the plush fabric. A sigh slipped from her throat. "Oh, this is nice," she said. She grabbed the other robe and hurried back to the bed. "Go ahead, try it."

Reluctantly, Cameron stood and slipped into the robe. Though it did feel nice on his naked skin, he much preferred seeing Sofie without clothes.

She grabbed the booklet of services from the bedside table and sat down on the bed. "I've never been to a spa before. Maybe we should try some services. Look at all these massages. Couples massage, chakra massage, hot-stone massage. I would love to have someone massage my feet."

"I can do that," he said. Cameron turned and grabbed her foot, then slowly began to knead it with his fingertips. She watched him, a playful smile twitching at her lips. "I better get a decent tip for this," he murmured.

She flopped back onto the bed. "I should really stop thinking about you and start focusing on Walter."

Cameron continued to rub her foot. "What's there to focus on? As soon as you get a few photos, you'll be finished, right?"

"I'd still like to know what he was up to out at that dig site."

"Maybe he'll tell me when we're talking business tonight."

"I just don't feel right about this. When I was doing police work, it was really easy to tell the bad guys from the good guys. But now, no matter what I do, everyone is going to get hurt. Stella Fredericks is going to hate her sister, Walter is going to hate Stella, and Vivian will probably end up hating both of them. And Walter and Stella have kids, two teenage girls. What's going to happen to them?"

"You were hired to do a job," he said.

"It just doesn't feel like a job. It feels like I'm destroying a family." She cursed softly. "Why do men have to cheat?"

"Haven't we discussed that subject before?" Cameron asked.

"Yes. But you didn't give me an answer. Why do men cheat?"

Cameron drew a deep breath, then pulled Sofie

into his lap. "Maybe they just haven't found that one woman who makes their life worth living. Maybe they're looking for someone who makes them want to be a better man, a woman who looks at them and sees the perfect body and thick hair and boyish smile that they had when they were younger."

"Does anyone find that?"

He nodded. "I think they do. I think my parents had that."

"I think mine do, too."

A long silence grew between them. "How's the foot? Feel good?"

She nodded. "Now do the other one. Maybe by the time you're finished I'll have this all figured out."

SOFIE STOOD IN the elevator, watching as the numbers above the door ticked down to the lobby. She was dressed in a pretty cotton halter dress that nearly reached her ankles and a pair of sandals decorated with turquoise beads and copper medallions. She'd seen them in the hotel dress shop and couldn't resist. After all, she needed more than just sexy red underwear to attract a man like Cameron.

With her hair freshly washed and her skin drenched in the spa's signature body lotion, she felt…beautiful.

"Do you remember the plan?" Sofie asked Cameron, who was standing beside her.

"I do. If Vivian is with him, you'll get some photos and then join us. If she isn't, you'll wait for me by the pool."

"Right."

The elevator door opened. Cameron took her hand and gave it a squeeze. "Don't worry."

"I'm not worried," she said lightly.

They went their separate ways, Sofie heading out to the pool while Cameron headed toward the bar. She stopped at the gift shop and bought a magazine, then wandered past the dress shop, considering another purchase.

She stepped inside and flipped through a rack of swimsuits before moving on to the dresses. When she found a pale blue sundress, she pulled it off the rack and held it up to herself in front of the mirror.

"That's a beautiful color on you, with your dark hair and eyes."

"Thanks," Sofie said, turning to smile at a slender blonde.

She had a large handbag slung over her shoulder and wore a voluminous cover-up over her swimsuit. "There are just so many pretty things in here. I've already bought two dresses and a bunch of their lingerie."

Sofie pulled another dress off the rack and held it up. "What do you think? This is nice."

"Oh, that is. Nice deep neckline. It'll show off a little cleavage." She giggled. "Nothing wrong with that."

"I guess not."

"Well, I'll leave you to your shopping," she said.

"Oh, by the way, I'm Vivian." She held out her hand. "Just in case we run into each other again."

Sofie's breath stopped in her throat. She pasted a smile on her face. "I'm Sofie," she said. "I—I was just going to go sit by the pool and have a drink. Would you like to join me?"

Vivian glanced at her watch. "Sure," she said. "My sweetie is having some kind of business meeting. He won't be done for a while. And I could certainly use a drink. All this healthy stuff is driving me crazy."

They walked out to the pool together and found a pair of lounge chairs away from a noisy group of women seated at a long table. Sofie relaxed into the comfortable cushions, and a moment later, a waiter stood beside them.

"I'll have a strawberry margarita," Vivian said. "With lots of sugar on the rim. And double tequila."

"A mojito," Sofie said. She closed her eyes, her mind spinning with topics of conversation. What kind of luck was this? Cameron was sitting inside with Walter, and here she was spending time with Vivian. "So, you're here with your husband?"

"Boyfriend. What about you?"

"I'm alone," Sofie said. "But I did meet a man this afternoon. Tall, dark and very handsome. We're going to have dinner together later."

"How long are you staying?" Vivian asked.

"I'm not sure. Until I feel renewed. The hydrotherapy makes my hip feel so much better, and the

Pilates helps keep me limber. If I could live here, I think I'd almost feel normal again."

"What happened?" Vivian asked. "I mean, if you don't mind my asking."

"Skiing accident. I broke my right leg. In three places. I'm just starting to feel better."

"I'm sorry. That's terrible. I don't do anything that might result in a broken limb. Except wear ridiculously high heels." She giggled. "That's the benefit of being with an older man," she said. "They prefer more sedentary activities."

"Your boyfriend is older?"

"Not that much older. Thirteen years. But he's just the sweetest thing. Believe me, nothing they say about older men is true. They can go all night long."

"How long have you been together?"

"Three years," she said. "Three wonderful years."

"That's a long time."

Vivian's smile faded. "I know. We plan to get married." She paused. "Just as soon as he divorces his wife."

"He's married?"

She nodded, her smile forced. "I mean, they barely speak anymore. But they have two daughters, and he's afraid that the girls will hate him if he leaves. There's also a prenup that will leave him with pretty much nothing. I have money, but he refuses to consider that I could support us."

"What does he do?"

"Oh, he has lots of businesses. Real estate and investments. He helps run the family car dealerships. And he's a city councilman in Albuquerque. That's why we have to keep our relationship quiet. It would be such a scandal."

"Yes," Sofie said. "I suppose it would."

"But everything will work out," she said. "I love him and he loves me. I just have to be patient." The waiter returned with their drinks, and Vivian took a long sip of her strawberry margarita. "I haven't even had a drink and I'm telling you my life story."

"I don't mind," Sofie said.

"Well, I guess you can't help who you love. I didn't want to fall in love with Walter, but I did. I just hope it all works out someday."

The waiter handed Sofie the mojito she'd ordered and she took a sip. This wasn't getting better; it was getting worse. She felt like a marriage counselor, not a private investigator. Was Stella really done with the marriage? If she was really only interested in the money, then maybe Walter and Vivian could have their happy ending. But once Stella found out that Vivian was the other woman, their relationship would be ruined. Or was it possible that she might be happy for her younger sister?

"Have you ever been in love?" Vivian asked in a wistful voice. "Oh, of course you have. What am I saying? Someone as beautiful as you are must have the guys lined up around the block."

"No," Sofie replied. "I thought I was in love once, but it wasn't right."

"Well, you never know when you're going to meet Mr. Right. He could be here. He could even be the man you met earlier today. I met Walter when I was seventeen. He was thirty so he was too old to even look at me. But I was in love with him from the very start." She clapped her hands. "Boom, just like that. Like I'd been struck by lightning."

Sofie couldn't help but like Vivian. She wasn't at all what Sofie had imagined her to be, some evil hussy out to ruin her sister's marriage. She was clearly in love with Walter, and though Sofie wasn't sure that her feelings were being returned in full measure, she had to think that Vivian believed they were.

The subject moved from men to interior decor as Vivian chatted about the work she was doing at the ranch. And when that subject was exhausted, she moved on to dogs, talking about the Border Collie she planned to buy just as soon as the house was re-decorated. Luckily, Vivian was such an animated conversationalist, Sofie barely had to do more than nod and reply.

"Where do you live?" Vivian finally asked.

Sofie paused, fighting the urge to tell the woman the truth, to warn her off and get her to think about how her actions would affect her sister and her nieces. "I—I live in San Francisco," she lied.

"I've always wanted to visit San Francisco, but I'm terrified of earthquakes. And tornadoes. And hurricanes. That's why I like living in the desert. Have you ever been in an earthquake?"

"Some small ones," Sofie said.

Vivian looked at her watch and then let out a tiny squeal. "Look at the time. I have to go." She gulped down the last of her drink and stood up, clutching her bag to her chest. "Let's do something tomorrow. Walter plans to go golfing. And I'd love to try the mud baths. We could go together. What's your room number?"

"I'm in 308," Sofie said.

"I'll call you. I promise. Mud baths. You and me."

Sofie watched Vivian disappear inside, then turned back to her drink. Until now, all the cases she'd worked with her uncle had been simple. This one seemed to be pretty much the same at first. But suddenly, it felt…personal.

"Hey." Cameron appeared from behind her and sat down on the chair that Vivian had abandoned. "What are you drinking?"

She handed him her glass. "Mojito. It's good. Very refreshing."

He took a swallow and then winced. "Mint?"

"It's an acquired taste. Finish it. You'll be hooked."

"We're having dinner with Walter and Vivian."

"Great. I just met Vivian. We had drinks together."

"Why do you look so…"

"So?"

"I don't know how to describe it. Perplexed?"

"I almost wanted to tell her everything. To warn

her about what's going to happen if she continues this affair with Walter. But then she told me how much she loves him, and I think maybe—maybe—they might belong together." Sofie groaned. "I can't believe I just said that. I'm turning into a sap."

Cameron laughed, then pulled her into a hug. "I promise, you're not a sap. You're just having trouble finding the bad guy in all of this."

"Walter. Walter is the bad guy. I've got no problem with that. He's cheating on his wife and daughters with his sister-in-law."

"Well, you might be right about that."

"What did he say?"

"It's what he didn't say that was interesting. We talked about commercial real estate and car washes and golf courses and strip malls. But then he brought up another opportunity that was sensitive in nature."

"That's what he called it? Sensitive?"

Cameron nodded. "He said he needed to put his hands on some decent money over the next few months and—"

"He's planning to leave Stella," she said.

"And he's had to get creative about how he did it. Income that couldn't be traced. A cash-only type of business opportunity."

"Creative? He's calling drug smuggling creative?"

"I'm not sure this is about drugs," Cameron replied. "I just don't think he'd put that out there to a complete stranger. I mean, I'm not sure he's even checked me out."

Sofie took a deep breath and smiled. "All right. Dinner with Walter and Vivian. This should be interesting."

6

To Cameron's surprise, the dinner wasn't as bad as he thought it would be. He and Sofie played their parts well, and any uneasiness was explained by the fact that they'd only met that morning.

The ladies had downed two bottles of champagne while he and Walter drank scotch. By the time they'd finished dessert, they were all laughing like old friends. He was surprised when Sofie pulled her cell phone from the pocket of her dress and held it out to Vivian. "Take a picture of us," she said, wrapping her arm around Cameron's shoulder.

"Oh, okay." Vivian aimed the phone at them both, and Cameron turned and pressed his lips to Sofie's cheek. "That's so cute," she cried. "Let me take one more. Sofie, you kiss him."

Sofie pressed her lips to Cameron's cheek, and he grinned for the camera.

"One more," Cameron said, this time turning and capturing Sofie's mouth in a sweet, fleeting kiss.

Then he held out his hand for the phone. "Let me take one of you two. Do you have your phone."

"Yes!" Vivian cried. "Sweetie, where's your phone?"

"I don't have a camera on my phone," Walter said.

"I can take one on my phone and send it to you," Sofie said.

"No, that's not necessary," Walter said.

"Oh, come on, sweetie," Vivian cried. "It will be fine. It's just us. Now smile."

Reluctantly, he did as she asked and Sofie took a few pictures. "Kiss," Sofie said.

Vivian grabbed Walter's face, and Sofie snapped the moment their lips touched.

"I'll send it to you," Sofie said. "Can you give me your cell-phone number and an email address?"

Vivian recited her number and email, and Sofie punched it into her phone.

"We should go," Cameron said. "It's getting late and—"

"Yes, it's getting late," Sofie agreed

Vivian gave them both a sly look. "You two run along. Sofie, I'll see you tomorrow. Don't forget. Mud baths."

Cameron stood and helped Sofie to her feet. "Walter, I'll be in touch. Vivian, it was a pleasure."

"I'll see you tomorrow," Sofie said.

They walked out of the restaurant toward the lobby, Sofie's hand tucked in the crook of Cameron's arm. "You are so smooth," he said. "I can't believe you got that photo."

"Four photos," Sofie said.

When the elevator doors opened, they walked inside. The moment the doors closed, Cameron pulled her into his arms and kissed her, pressing her back against the mirrored wall. "Do you have any idea how difficult it is to keep from touching you?" he murmured.

"You did a very good job hiding your thoughts," she said.

He ran his hand along her thigh, then slipped it beneath the hem of her dress. Slowly, he smoothed it between her legs and Sofie gasped.

"It's a very short ride to the third floor," she said.

"Not short enough," he said, capturing her mouth again.

By the time the doors opened again, Cameron was frantic to possess her. He grabbed her hand and pulled her along to the room, then fumbled with the key card. Sofie took it from his hand and opened the door. With his hands on her waist, they stumbled inside.

"I think we have some unfinished business," he said.

"Business or pleasure?"

"All right. Pleasure."

There was nothing else in the world he needed at that moment. In truth, Cameron would have given up everything he owned for this chance to be with Sofie. He needed to know how deep this connection ran.

In the past, he'd been so careful not to let emotion rule his pursuit of pleasure. It was about the physical release and nothing deeper. But with Sofie, he felt more than just passion. There was affection and respect and contentment. His world felt perfectly in balance when he was with her.

They teased each other as they kissed, tugging at clothes and discarding them piece by piece. With each inch of flesh revealed, they tasted and touched, as if discovering each other for the very first time. And when they'd managed to eliminate all the barriers between them, they fell onto the bed, their mouths meeting again in a desperate kiss.

His hands skimmed over her naked body, memorizing each curve, each delicious swell of flesh. Would there come a day when he'd have to rely on his mind to conjure images of her? She was close to him now, but how long would that last?

Right now, he couldn't think about the future. He wanted to savor this moment, to make it more than either one of them ever expected. Cameron kissed a path from her mouth to her shoulder, then worked his way down to her breasts.

She arched against him as his tongue teased at each nipple, bringing it to a hard peak before moving on. When she slipped her fingers through his hair, he followed her cues, lingering at certain places for a bit longer. But when he reached the spot between her legs, her hands slid to his shoulders, her palms pressed against him as if the pleasure was too much to take.

He slipped his finger inside of her as he teased her with his tongue, and Sofie groaned, writhing beneath him. Cameron kept it up until he was certain of her responses. She wanted more yet wouldn't let him bring her to completion.

When he pressed a kiss to her belly, she reached out and retrieved a condom from the box he'd purchased earlier that evening. With deft fingers, she sheathed him, then drew him up until he was settled between her legs.

Cameron braced himself above her, watching her reactions. He smoothed her hair away from her face and kissed her softly as he slowly pushed inside her. Her breath caught and then slipped out on a long sigh.

When he was buried to the hilt, Sofie opened her eyes and smiled. Cameron drew her into another kiss, desperate to taste her, to experience every sensation that she offered.

Sofie wrapped her arms around his neck, pulling him close as he began to move inside her. Every nerve in his body was alive with sensation, and his only need was to get closer to her.

He grabbed her waist and rolled her over until she sat on top of him, her legs straddling his hips. Her dark hair tumbled around her face as she leaned forward and then sank back. And when she paused, he felt himself dancing on the edge of control. Her body was open to his touch, and his fingertips drifted from her breast to the damp crease between her legs.

When he touched her there, she began to move again, slowly at first. Watching her come down on him was impossibly erotic, and though he couldn't see where they were joined, he could imagine it. When her breath caught, he knew he'd discovered the secret to her release.

From that moment on, they raced toward their climaxes, Sofie rocking above him, her hands pressed against his chest, Cameron urging her on. It was hard to believe they'd only known each other for a few days. His need for her was already overwhelming, and it didn't show any signs of diminishing.

Cameron felt the first signs of her orgasm as she moaned softly. Sofie seemed to grow slicker with each stroke, and he waited for the first shudder and then the wave of spasms. Her expression was focused, her brow furrowed, and then without warning, she gasped.

Sofie's body dissolved into deep and visible tremors, the sensation a delicious counterpoint to his own need. Cameron wrapped his hands around her waist and pulled her beneath him, burying himself deep inside her as his own release overwhelmed him.

When his pulse had slowed and his body recovered, Cameron rolled onto his side and pulled her leg over his hip, still caught inside her warmth. "Don't move," he whispered.

"I'm not sure I could if I wanted to," Sofie said, dragging her finger across his bottom lip. Suddenly, she winced. "Ow. Cramp."

"Where?"

She pointed to her hip, and Cameron gently massaged it, moving down to her thigh and back up again. "Better?"

"I need to work a little harder on my rehab. I have a therapist in Albuquerque, but this wasn't exactly on my exercise list."

"It can't be bad for you," Cameron said. "You look very...healthy right now." He paused. "You really want to go back, don't you?"

"It's what I do best."

Cameron shook his head. "No. This is definitely what you do best."

"And what do you do best, besides this?" Sofie asked.

"I used to think I was a damn good boat builder," Cameron said. "But I've been away from it for six days now, and I haven't thought about it at all."

"It's been a very strange couple of days," Sofie said. "I wasn't even going to have lunch at Millie's that day, but I'd been thinking about pie. Lucky thing."

"So it's pie that brought us together. Not fate or destiny?"

"Yes, it was pie."

"So what's next, after this case?" he asked. "Am I going to have to find a real job?"

"What do you want to do?" Sofie asked.

"This," he said. "I'm quite good at it, don't you think?"

"Besides this," she said. "You don't get paid for this."

"Maybe I should start charging you."

"Now, that would be a way to make a living," Sofie said. "What kind of rates are you considering?"

"How much do you think I'm worth?"

"Well, I'm not sure. Depends if you charge by the hour or by the amount of pleasure you manage to give me. It's quality versus quantity."

"I suppose this is something we're going to have to discuss. Maybe even negotiate. I never really thought about a career as a gigolo, but if my prospects for respectable work aren't that good around Vulture Creek, I may have to consider it."

"So I would pay you to provide sexual favors?" she asked.

Cameron nodded. "I'd work for food and a place to sleep."

"All right," she said. "I suppose it's something I could think about. As long as you include a daily foot massage, I think it might work out."

"Would I have to call you 'boss'?"

"Of course," she said. "That would be a requirement."

Though they hadn't mentioned the word *future,* they'd managed to address it without having to make any commitments. Though it wasn't an honest job, it was certainly something he could be passionate about. And he'd find a way to make some spending money. He was good with his hands and knew how to wield a hammer and saw.

"So, what will I call you?" Sofie asked. "Houseboy? Sex slave? Stud muffin?"

"None of those seem to suit me." Cameron kissed her softly. "But I'm sure you'll think of something."

SOFIE OPENED HER EYES to the morning sun that poured into the window of the room. Pushing up on her elbow, she brushed her tangled hair out of her eyes and looked down at the man sleeping next to her.

She expected to feel some sort of guilt or remorse for what they'd done, but Sofie didn't feel anything but complete and utter satisfaction. So what if they'd only known each other for a few days? They were both adults, both perfectly able to make decisions about their sex lives. They'd decided to indulge their desires and it had been wonderful. There was nothing left to say.

But there was plenty left to do, Sofie mused. They had just over five weeks left, and if they chose to spend that time together, there would be many more nights just like the last one.

Sofie knew she shouldn't get too attached to Cameron. One day, he'd return to Seattle. And all the plans she'd made for her future didn't include a man. But for now, as long as he was with her, she was going to think about the present, about how happy he made her and how good she felt about herself when they were together.

Maybe someday she'd get back everything she'd lost. All her dreams would finally be restored. But right now, she had everything she needed, and that was more than enough.

Sofie sighed, her thoughts wandering to the case. She had her evidence, proof that Walter had a mistress. And though she suspected something else was going on with him, there was no reason she had to take things any further.

Why not just turn the pictures over to Stella and let the woman deal with the fallout? Sofie and Cameron could move on, maybe spend more time enjoying each other.

She felt a surge of guilt and brushed it aside. Sofie was usually able to distance herself from the individuals involved in her investigations, to look at the facts objectively, unemotionally. But there was something about this situation that she found upsetting.

There were very deep emotions at play between Vivian and Walter and Stella. Destroying a family, a loving relationship and the lives of five people was not something Sofie wanted on her conscience.

She flopped back down on the pillow and closed her eyes. Was there a way to repair the damage already done, to make this case…disappear? Sofie bit back a groan. What difference did it make? Why couldn't she just do the job she was hired for and get it over with?

Rolling onto her side, she tucked her arm under her head and silently observed the man sleeping beside her. Something had changed inside her. She was no longer able to see the world in black and white, good and evil, right and wrong. Suddenly, there were all kinds of grays.

Had Cameron done that? Or was it simply the lingering aftereffects of having her life come apart at the seams? She used to be so sure of what she wanted. She'd pursued her dreams with a single-minded purpose. And then, after they'd been snatched away from her, she'd made a vow to get it all back again.

But she'd never considered that there might be something else out there for her, just waiting for her to discover it. Her mother had whispered something similar to her when she'd first opened her eyes in the hospital, but it had made Sofie even more determined to recapture what she'd lost.

She ran her palm up Cameron's arm, pressing her lips to his shoulder. Maybe she ought to do what Cameron was doing—just move someplace new and try out a different life for six weeks. Find a job, meet new people, imagine that there might be other possibilities.

Cameron stirred and a moment later he opened his eyes. He smiled as he rolled onto his side to face her. "Morning," he said. "It is morning, isn't it?"

Sofie nodded. "It is. It's about nine."

"Did you sleep well?"

"I did. I was pretty exhausted. And I'd had a little too much champagne. But I feel great now."

"Should we get some breakfast? Or do you want to spend the rest of the day in bed?"

Sofie sat up, pulling the sheet around her naked body. "You know what I'd like to do? Let's just get out of here. Let's forget the case for a day or two and have some fun."

"Can we do that?"

She smiled. "Sure we can. I'm the boss. We can do whatever I say we can."

"So what's the plan?"

"I don't know. We'll figure it out as we go along."

"All right. Do you want the shower first or can I have it?"

"We could share it," Sofie said.

"If we share the shower, we'll never get out of here," Cameron said. "You go and I'll order us some breakfast."

She started to crawl out of bed, but Cameron grabbed her hand and pulled her back against his body. "Wait. Not quite yet."

"What?" Sofie asked.

He kissed her softly, then smoothed her hair back from her face. "You look really pretty in the morning," he said. "I like waking up with you."

"This is really strange," Sofie said, shaking her head. "Not in a bad way. It's just different. I—I like it, too."

"All right, then." He kissed her again. "Now you

can get out of bed and walk to the bathroom. But leave the sheet here and walk really slowly, all right?"

Sofie slipped out of his embrace and strolled toward the bathroom, running her hands through her tangled hair as she walked. She glanced over her shoulder and found him watching her, his arms linked behind his head as he leaned back against the headboard of the bed.

"What do you think? Could I make a living at the Bunny Shack? I'm thinking I need to consider some new career options."

"No," he said. "No Bunny Shack for you."

She grabbed the robe from the hook as she walked past, then stepped into the spacious bathroom. The marble shower, the size of a walk-in closet, was made for at least two people. Sofie turned on the water, and it poured from a huge showerhead above her.

Tossing the robe aside, she stepped inside and closed her eyes, letting the warm water rush over her body. Between the French bed linens and the soft cotton robes and the drenching shower, she'd come to enjoy every pleasurable sensation the spa had to offer, including those that Cameron had provided.

Sofie made a mental note to treat herself more often. It was surprising how these little pleasures made her feel much more feminine…even beautiful. As she began to lather her hair, she felt his hands slip around her waist.

"I thought you were going to wait," Sofie said, wiping soap out of her eyes.

Her breath caught in her throat as his lips touched hers. Her knees buckled and her body grew soft in his embrace. The sensations racing through her were just too delicious—the warmth of his skin against hers, the water running over her back, the tug of his fingers as they tangled in her soapy hair.

Her lips parted and he took more, deepening the kiss until it became an unspoken communication between them. He was asking her to surrender, to admit that she wanted him as much as he wanted her. Sofie moaned softly, then wrapped her arms around his neck, pressing her naked body against his.

His skin was slick and she skimmed her hands across his chest, then moved up to his shoulders. Sofie's fingers twisted in the hair at his nape, and he growled softly as his hands slipped around her hips to her backside. He picked her up and wrapped her legs around his waist.

How was this possible? she wondered. She couldn't seem to stop herself. They'd met a few days ago, and yet every minute of that time had been spent contemplating just this.

He was so beautiful, so perfect. And to have the chance to touch such beauty was something she wasn't going to refuse. Cameron was a man who took what he wanted, confident that she wanted the same. He brushed aside her insecurities and fears as if they didn't exist. There was only an intense and undeniable desire to possess.

He ran his hands over her slick skin, exploring

every inch of exposed flesh before he moved on. Sofie smiled as he stepped beneath the shower and rinsed the soap from her hair. Her morning shower had always been a very ordinary way to start the day. But this was something quite different.

To Sofie, it was the most natural thing in the world to cast aside the last of her inhibitions. She wasn't rational; she wasn't considering consequences. From the moment their bodies touched, she was acting on instinct, something so primal that it pushed her forward, past any bounds of propriety.

She couldn't stop and she didn't want to. His pleasure was hers. And whatever they shared together, from moment to moment, seemed like nothing less than pure perfection.

"I guess we're going to be staying a little longer," she murmured.

THE JEEP SPED THROUGH the desert, the highway a ribbon of black asphalt that captured the noonday heat. Cameron glanced over at Sofie. She sat in the passenger seat, her dark hair whipping in the wind, her face turned up to the sun. He reached over and ran his fingers over her shoulder. She turned and smiled at him.

"Are you going to tell me where we're going?"

"We're going to visit my ancestors," she said.

"I'm going to meet your family?"

Sofie laughed. "No. Well, the spirits of my family. My mother's family." She pointed to a road sign. "Turn left up here."

"'Bandelier National Monument,'" he read. They pulled up to a ranger station and paid the fee to get in, then drove into a parking area.

"This is Anasazi culture for beginners," she said. "If you're interested in more, I'll take you out to Chaco Canyon. It's more remote and more difficult to hike. I kind of like Bandelier better. It's like a secret spot, hidden in the canyon."

They got out of the car and strolled to the trailhead. "It's beautiful," Cameron said, taking in the stunning landscape. "What's here?"

"Cliff dwellings. And there are kivas, which are like ceremonial buildings. There were people living here about 10,000 years ago, long before the great civilizations in Greece and Rome and five thousand years before the Egyptian civilization began. Then, sometime around 1200, the civilization collapsed. No one really knows why. Some people think there was a drought that forced the people to move out of the area to find food."

They walked the loop, Sofie serving as tour guide, explaining each site and its significance to the culture. Though Cameron knew he was Irish, he knew very little about his ancestors. But Sofie was steeped in her Native American roots.

They walked along the bank of the river, shaded by trees that he didn't recognize. And then they ascended four ladders up at least a hundred feet, to a cluster of apartments built into the cliffside.

Sofie thought nothing of the climb, scampering up the ladders as if she had absolutely no fear. When they reached the top, Cameron stood under a rock overhang, looking down at the river.

He had never seen anything like it. It was magnificent, awe-inspiring and strangely solemn. Though he didn't have a drop of Native American blood in him, he understood the significance of the spot. The combination of the sky and the mountain, the pine trees and the pink cliff created an image he'd never forget.

"It's amazing," he said.

She slipped her arm through his. "I know. I can feel them, their spirits. I'm not a religious person, but when I come here, I understand that there's something bigger than me out there."

He bent close and brushed a kiss across her lips. "Thank you for bringing me."

"I knew you'd like it. There aren't any dinosaurs, but—"

"It's better. I used to have this book when I was a kid. It was called *Lost Civilizations.* I read that thing from cover to cover. I'd imagine I was Indiana Jones and discover all these amazing places. Machu Picchu. Atlantis. Petra. Troy. I wanted to see them all."

"Have you ever had a chance to do any exploring?"

Cameron shook his head. "No. There never seemed to be time. I just don't take vacations. And when I do take time off, I usually sail somewhere. But this— this makes me want to see the world."

They finished the loop, taking their time at each spot, then strolled back to the parking area. Sofie pointed to the gift shop, and they walked inside the air-conditioned building and sighed.

"You want something to drink?" she asked.

"You know, I haven't paid for anything since I arrived. I'm starting to feel like a kept man."

"You're a cheap date," she said.

"Well, someday, you're going to have to let me return the favor."

They grabbed a few bottles of water, then wandered through the gift shop. Sofie pulled him over to a display case and pointed to some small pots painted with black-and-white geometric designs. "My mother made these," she said.

"Your mother?"

"Yeah. She's a potter. She designs reproductions of Anasazi bowls and pots and ladles."

"I'd like to meet your family," Cameron said. He wasn't sure why he'd made the request, but after spending the afternoon with Sofie, he wanted to know even more about her.

"No, I don't think that would be a good idea."

"Why not?"

"You met Tony. Now multiply that by one hundred. And Tony is the quiet one in the family. The one that doesn't stick his nose in anyone else's business. And—"

"Yeah, all right. But I'm a nice guy. I could handle it."

She sent him a sideways glance. "Well, my niece is having her *quinceañera* next weekend. You could meet the whole family then."

"Quinceañera?" he said.

"Her fifteenth birthday party. It's a big, big deal. There'll be music and dancing and lots of food, as well as very loud relatives who will ask you all kinds of embarrassing questions."

"All right," Cameron said. If that was what it took to learn more about Sofie, then he was willing to risk a little embarrassment. "So what kind of questions?"

"My aunt Vera once asked my brother's father-in-law whether he had hair plugs or just a bad toupee. He had neither. And my aunt Lola told my cousin's boyfriend that if he wore his pants any tighter, his ability to father children would be in serious jeopardy. My family just says whatever comes into their heads."

"Well, I have good hair and I don't wear tight pants."

"Oh, it will be something else. How much money do you make? Have you ever had a social disease? How often do you go to church?"

"Sofie, I like spending time with you. And I want to meet your family. No matter how crazy they are, it's not going to change how I feel about you."

"And how do you feel about me?" Sofie asked.

He grabbed her hand and kissed her fingertips.

"I like you. A lot. I'm thinking that you're kind of my girlfriend."

"Don't you think you're moving a little fast?" she teased. "We just met."

He shook his head and leaned closer. "But we have slept together. And I've seen you naked. And we took a shower together. And you've done some—"

"All right," Sofie said. "I'll think about it."

"I'll do my best to convince you."

He grabbed her hand, and they walked out into the afternoon heat. After they got into the Jeep, Cameron reached over and pulled her into another kiss. Finally, they'd reached a point where he was able to touch her and kiss her without having to hesitate. She wanted him as much as he wanted her.

Though Cameron had no idea where this was all going or when it would end, he was happy. Genuinely happy. And he wasn't sure that he'd ever felt quite this way. Somehow, he sensed that his life was changing, shifting, moving in a whole new direction. He didn't know how but he knew why.

He was falling in love with Sofie Reyes.

7

THE MUSIC FROM the *banda* filled the night air and drifted into the house. Sofie stood on the back porch and stared out at the crowd gathered in her brother's backyard. Brightly colored paper lanterns were strung from the trees. A feast of traditional Mexican dishes was laid out beneath a small tent, and one of her cousins was mixing drinks on an old card table.

If she had any worries at all about Cameron fitting in, they had all disappeared just moments after he arrived. Strangely, her brothers welcomed him with a cup of beer, and her father, though distant at first, had gradually warmed up enough to invite him to play a Reyes family variation of boccie ball.

The door opened behind her, and a moment later, Sofie's mother joined her at the railing of the back porch. "Your friend seems to be getting along well," Talie Reyes said.

"Papa has him playing that silly game. You know

they change the rules as they go along. Wait until they find out he has no money to gamble."

"Oh, I'm sure they'll lend him whatever he needs," her mother teased. She slipped her hand around Sofie's waist. "Come help me clean up the kitchen. Elena has enough to worry about keeping all of Gabby's friends in line. And the girls all seem to be quite taken with your guest."

Sofie smiled as she noticed the cluster of teenage girls watching the game from a nearby picnic table. Though she accepted that Cameron was good-looking, she'd never really seen the effect he could have on the opposite sex—beyond what he did to her.

But he'd been impossibly charming to everyone he'd met. And nearly every female at the party, from her niece Gabby to her ninety-year-old great-aunt, had something positive to say about Sofie's sexy friend.

She turned and walked into the kitchen. Her mother handed her a dish towel and then went back to washing dishes. It was a scene that Sofie had replayed every night since she was able to hold a dish. She and her mother at the sink, cleaning up after supper while her older brothers went off to spend their evenings in more enjoyable pursuits.

"I was surprised you came today," her mother said. "And that you brought your friend. Lately, you've been avoiding family parties."

"I know. I just didn't want to have to talk about the accident. Or my plans for the future."

Her mother laughed. "Well, Sofia, you certainly found a creative way to change the subject."

"Yes. He does make a nice distraction, doesn't he?"

"I thought your gift to Gabby was lovely. That girl would dip herself in pink if she could."

"She emailed me a photo of her dress. I figured if she liked it enough for her *quinceañera* dress, I'd be safe with a pink makeup case." Sofie turned and leaned back against the edge of the counter. "Do you remember my *quinceañera?*"

Her mother shook her head. "I had to pay you to wear a dress. And instead of gifts, you made everyone donate money toward new Kevlar vests for the police department. Your grandmother Reyes was beside herself. Of course, your father was so proud." Her mother handed her a plate. "It's been a while since we've done this. I've missed it."

"Why didn't you ever have one of the boys help you with the dishes? Why was it always my job?" Sofie asked.

"I suppose it was the only way I got to spend any time with you," her mother said. "I learned pretty early on that you were your father's girl. I guess I just wanted to have you to myself at least once a day."

Sofie had always bristled at the fact that she was forced into domestic duty, when she was more interested in doing whatever her brothers were doing.

But suddenly, she realized how much she and her mother had missed. They'd never shopped for pretty dresses or read fairy tales or played dress-up. From the moment Sofie took her first step, she'd begun following her brothers.

"I'm sorry," Sofie murmured. "I know I wasn't the daughter I should have been. Or the daughter you wanted."

"Oh, sweetheart, don't be. I never resented your relationship with your father and your brothers. They helped you grow up into a fine, strong woman, and that's all I ever dreamed for you." She smiled. "Besides, I knew there would come a time when you'd need me. When we'd share some common ground."

"Like now?" Sofie said.

Her mother nodded. "Now. And when you got married and had children. And when those children were sick. And when they left for their first day of school. You and I still have a lot to share." She handed Sofie another dish. "So, tell me about this man of yours."

"He's not mine, Mama. He just...dropped into my life. And now I'm not sure I want him to leave."

"How long have you known him?"

"Ten days." Sofie groaned and buried her face in the dish towel. "I can't believe I just said that. Ten days? What's wrong with me?"

"Oh, I suspect you might be in love," her mother said. She took the towel from Sofie and wiped her hands, then drew her daughter along toward the kitchen table. "Sit."

Her mother fetched a pitcher of sangria from the refrigerator and poured them both a glass, then sat down beside her. Though her mother was nearly sixty, she still had a youthful beauty about her. Her complexion was unlined and her jet-black hair, bound in a long braid, was touched with gray at her temples. She dressed as she always had, in a mix of designer casual and Hopi-influenced accessories, the picture of a successful artist and businesswoman.

Sofie had always looked up to her father, but her mother had made an amazing life for herself, too. Natalie Humatewa was the only daughter of a single mom. Raised on the reservation, she learned traditional Hopi crafts from her grandmother. After graduating from the Native American high school in Phoenix, she'd been awarded a full scholarship to study art at Santa Fe University. She ran a successful art gallery, taught several college classes in Native American art and was well respected in the business community. And she had raised six children.

Why had it taken Sofie this long to recognize her mother for all she was? Tears pushed at the corners of her eyes, and Sofie covered her face with her hands. "I don't know what I'm doing," she said. "I'm sorry. I—I thought I would—"

"Sofie, this doesn't have to be so difficult. This man seems to like you exactly the way you are," Talie said. "I see the way he looks at you. With affection and pride. All you have to do is be yourself."

"I'm not sure who that is anymore. The person I was for the first twenty-six years of my life is gone."

"No. She's still right here in front of me. My grandmother used to tell me that I must always live my life from beginning to end. You would do well to heed her advice, Sofia."

"What does that mean?" she asked.

"This is not the end, darling. You have so much more in front of you. And if you spend all your time mourning what might have been, you won't be able to see anything else through your tears. You'll miss all the wonderful things that are about to be."

Sofie brushed the damp streaks from her face. "I think I might be falling in love with him, Mama."

"I think you might be right."

"But he lives in Seattle and I live here."

"You'll have to work that out. It's your life. Don't let little things like that stand in your way. Your grandmother Reyes disapproved of me when your father and I first met, but I didn't let that stop me from marrying him."

"Really? Why didn't she like you?"

"I wasn't Catholic. I had plans for a career and wasn't satisfied simply being a housewife. But for your papa, it was love at first sight. He went home the night after meeting me and told his mother he'd met his future wife. She wasn't amused."

"How did you know you were in love with Papa?" Sofie asked.

"Oh, he made me laugh," she said, smiling. "I was very serious back then. Very focused. I had a plan for my life, and getting married wasn't part of it."

"Like me," Sofie murmured.

"I remember the first time I knew. I was upset about a teacher that I had for one of my art classes, and your father was trying to cheer me up. He took a couple of my paintbrushes and put them up his nose, then proceeded to explain to me, in a very serious voice, why he thought he was a better artist than me because he could paint with his nose. I went from tears to laughter in a heartbeat, and then I couldn't stop laughing."

"That sounds like Papa," Sofie said.

"He still makes me laugh. There will come a time, Sofie, when the clouds will part and the answer will be as clear as the sky. And then you'll know what to do. For now, just be patient."

Sofie stood and moved to her mother, then wrapped her arms around Talie's neck. "I love you, Mama."

"I love you, daughter." She kissed Sofie's cheek, then held her face between her hands. "Why don't you go out and ask that nice young man to dance? Don't let your father and uncles scare him off."

Sofie shook her head. "He wouldn't get scared off. He's the kind of guy who sticks, no matter what."

"Well, that's not a bad quality to find in a man," her mother said.

Sofie wandered to the door, then gave her mother a smile before she stepped outside. She found Cameron in the middle of an argument over the game, hunched over two of the balls and measuring the space between them with a broken yardstick.

Sofie bent down and grabbed his hand, then handed her father the yardstick. "Let's dance," she said.

"You can't take him now," her father said. "We're in the middle of a game. And we're winning."

"He's my date," she said.

"Wait," her father said, frowning. "I thought he was just a friend." He looked at Cameron, his eyes narrowing. "You're dating?"

Cameron shrugged. "This is the first I've heard about it," he said.

"Well, I've decided," Sofie said. "We're officially dating. And if anyone has a problem with that, you can take it up with me later." She held tight to Cameron's hand and pulled him along to the dance floor. Most of the *banda* was gathered in the food tent for a break, while a pair of guitarists played a soft ballad.

Cameron pulled her into his arms, holding her right hand against his chest as they moved to the beat. "I didn't realize you could dance," she murmured

"Neither did I," Cameron said. "It's not something I've done very often. Tell me if I'm doing it wrong, okay?"

She stepped back and saw a hint of worry in his eye. "You're doing pretty well."

"Maybe if I'm a moving target, you father won't be able to shoot me."

"I only outlined the parameters of our relationship. Everyone seemed to be curious, and I was tired of them speculating."

"At least you didn't tell him we were sleeping together."

"I'm not a fool," she said. "Although he must realize that I'm not a virgin anymore."

He leaned close and whispered in her ear, "Even under torture, I'd never reveal your secrets."

Sofie groaned softly as he pulled her a bit closer. She did have a few secrets, a few things she did in the bedroom that drove him wild, and Sofie felt a bit naughty thinking of those things while at a family function. But no one could see how the feel of his body against hers was sending delicious sensations racing through her and how she was tempted to open his shirt and press her lips to his naked chest.

They danced through the first song and into the next, lost in their own world. But Sofie was aware of the stares that followed them around the dance floor. Everyone at the party was curious about this new man in her life.

"I feel like we're in a fishbowl," Sofie said.

He glanced around, then chuckled. "You're the

most beautiful woman at this party. And I'm the guy who brought you."

"But that's not why they're staring. They've all been worried I'd die a spinster. Or that I preferred girls to boys."

"I suppose I could assure them of your preference for guys," Cameron said. "In fact, I could even provide photographic proof."

"I think, for now, we ought to keep that part of our relationship to ourselves. Let my father have his delusions."

He bent close, his lips soft on her ear. "I never kiss and tell. You can count on me."

She felt a shiver skitter down her spine as her breath caught. It was just a simple statement. Two sentences. But it was the moment that her mother had told her would come, the moment that she knew Cameron was the one she wanted.

This man was kind and loyal. He was her lover and her friend. And though he'd never been tested, she knew with every atom of her being that she could trust him with her life.

But was she ready to admit that out loud? Or was that a secret she'd keep to herself a bit longer?

THE COOL, QUIET interior of Sofie's Albuquerque apartment was a welcome relief from the raucous noise of the *quinceañera* celebration. Cameron closed the door behind him, then watched as Sofie dropped her keys and a container of birthday cake on the table next to the door.

Though he'd enjoyed his stay in the old Airstream, he was happy to have the comforts of a real home, if only for a night. His mind flashed to an image of his place in Seattle, wondering what it might be like to have Sofie in surroundings familiar to him. Sofie lying in his bed—or curled up on his living-room sofa—or making coffee in his kitchen. Each new possibility was more tempting than the last.

But would that fantasy ever become reality? Somehow, he couldn't imagine Sofie ever leaving the desert for the lush green landscape and salty sea air in Seattle. This was where she belonged. Close to her family and her culture.

Cameron held his breath as she reached down and grabbed the hem of her cotton dress. She pulled it over her head and tossed it onto the sofa, then continued on into what Cameron assumed was her bedroom, kicking off her shoes along the way.

By the time he'd reached the door, she was lying on the bed in just her underwear, staring at the ceiling. "Sometimes my family can exhaust me."

"I had fun tonight," he said. "It was nice to meet everyone."

"You were a big hit," Sofie replied. "I think they all liked you. I know my mother did."

"Did she say that?" Cameron asked.

Sofie rolled onto her side, bracing her head on her hand. "Yes."

"She's a beautiful woman. You look a lot like her."

Sofie patted the mattress beside her. "Come here, my boyfriend."

As he crossed the room, Cameron slowly unbuttoned his shirt. He stretched out beside her, and Sofie pushed the cotton fabric away from his chest. She pressed her lips to his neck. "I wanted to do this when we were dancing." She reached for the front button of his jeans and flipped it open. "It works much better in bed, don't you think?"

"I could get used to your bed." He smoothed his hands over her hair, the strands like silk in his fingers. "It's much more comfortable than the Airstream. Now that the case is done in Vulture Creek, are we going to work on another one here in Albuquerque?"

"We're going to take a break," Sofie said. "And have some fun."

"Did you give the photos to your uncle tonight?"

"No." Sofie shook her head. "I don't want to talk about the case right now."

"Isn't your uncle going to wonder about what's going on?"

"He asked me how things were progressing, right before we left tonight. I told him I didn't have anything new to report."

"But you do," he said. "You have the photos and a name and a location."

She drew a slow breath. "I know. But I'm not sure I want to use it. Who am I to put myself in the middle of this mess? Don't you think they should be able to work this out without any outside interference?"

"But that's what you're getting paid for, Sof. Stella Fredericks hired you to find out if her husband was cheating on her. And you have the answer."

"But don't you think it would be much better if Walter just sat down and talked to Stella? He should be the one to tell her about Vivian, not me. Or maybe Vivian should talk to her sister. This is just a bad situation, and I think having a stranger in the middle of it is just going to make it worse."

"Why the change of heart?"

"Vivian seems to genuinely love Walter. And he seems to love her. Maybe the circumstances aren't perfect, but there might be a chance that they can make each other happy. No, I don't think Walter cheating on his wife is acceptable, but now that he's done it, he needs to own up and make things right, for everyone involved."

"What are you going to do?"

Sofie thought about it for a moment, then flopped back onto the bed. "As soon as I know, I'll discuss it with my faithful assistant. Until then, I think he should kiss me."

Cameron touched his lips to hers in a sweet, lingering kiss. "All right, boss. Whatever you say. I've got your back. And your front."

Sofie smiled, then pulled him into a deeper kiss, raking her fingers through his hair and sending desire snaking through his veins. They'd been together for about a week and a half, and it still seemed so new and exciting.

Usually by this time Cameron would have grown restless and begun to question whether he needed a woman in his life at all. But Sofie had managed to work her way into his heart, and there didn't seem to be any reason to believe she'd be going anywhere soon.

They had four more weeks. He'd be happy to spend the rest of that time in her bed, but if they didn't work another case, he had to find some way to make a living. He couldn't mooch off of Sofie for an entire month.

"There is something I need to talk to you about," he said.

"Is it about the fact that you're still dressed and I'm not?" Sofie asked.

"No." Cameron sat up and pulled off his shirt. "Your brother mentioned that he's been wanting to do some remodeling in his kitchen. Since I need a job, I told him that I might be available."

"Which brother?"

"Carlos? I guess he lives here in Albuquerque?"

"Ugh, his kitchen is horrible," she said. "But you don't have to work."

"I can't continue to sponge off of you, Sofie. You've paid for everything since we met. I'm starting to feel guilty. Carlos said he'd pay me ten dollars an hour, which is more than I could make slinging burgers at Millie's. And I'm good with my hands, so—"

"Yes, you are very good with your hands." Sofie reached down and grabbed his left one, placing it on her breast. "I thought you were going to be my sex slave."

"As much as I'd totally dominate at that job, I think I'd probably have to spend everything I earn on condoms. And sad to say, I might not be up to the demands of round-the-clock sex."

"I suppose we can't stay in this apartment all day long," Sofie said.

"And I was thinking I should probably find a place to stay. I don't want to impose on—"

"No," Sofie said. "You'll stay here. I want you here. If you're feeling guilty, you can buy groceries every now and then. Or maybe cook a meal. Or do laundry. But you don't have to pay rent."

"All right," Cameron said, satisfied that they'd laid out the terms to his satisfaction. Though he wasn't technically in Vulture Creek, he was close enough. He'd had a job and a place to sleep in Vulture Creek, but now he was moving on to bigger and better things.

"All right," Sofie repeated. "Now take off the rest of your clothes and come to bed."

Cameron kicked out of his boots, then stripped off his jeans and socks.

"Boxers, too," she said.

When he was naked, he waited, watching a smile twitch at the corners of her mouth.

"Better?" he asked.

"The best," she murmured. "So, you wanna dance?"

He sank down onto the bed beside her, pulling her against his body and smoothing his hands over the curves of her backside. This was how it should be, Cameron thought to himself. Pure and utter contentment. He didn't want to be anywhere else, with anyone else.

She reached between their bodies and touched him, the contact sending a wave of pleasure crashing over him. It didn't take much to bring him to the edge, but Cameron had learned to control his reactions, knowing that better things would come if he'd take her with him.

When he couldn't bear it anymore, he pulled her against him, her backside tucked into the curve of his body. He had complete access to every inch of her flesh, and he ran his hands from her breasts to her belly to the soft juncture of her thighs.

The satin bra and panties found a place on the floor beside his clothes, and as she arched against him, Cameron found the damp spot between her legs. He knew what she liked, knew exactly how to caress her to a shuddering release.

But Sofie wanted more than just his touch. After he sheathed himself, she reached back and guided him inside her slick heat. Though he was familiar with the destination, the sensations were entirely new and overwhelmingly erotic.

She moved against him, and Cameron grabbed her hips to stop her, taking a long moment to regain his control. When he was ready, he drew back, then plunged deep. Sofie moaned softly, her fingers still tangled in his hair.

He kissed her on her shoulder, then moved to the sweet curve of her neck, his teeth grazing her silken skin. This was the woman he never knew he needed—or wanted—or loved. Had he not come to Vulture Creek, he might have gone his whole life waiting for her.

Now that he'd found her, Cameron wasn't sure he'd ever be able to let her go. And though a future might look impossible, he had to believe that everything would work out. People fell in love every day, and there were always complications. But love was supposed to conquer all.

The hard part was over. They'd met. Against all odds, they'd found each other in a world of millions. Cameron would make it work. He had no choice.

As Sofie reached the edge, Cameron let his body respond, and when he felt the first spasms of her orgasm, he buried himself deep inside of her, his surrender inevitable.

She fell asleep still curled against him, Cameron's arms wrapped around her waist, his chin resting on her shoulder. As he listened to her soft, even breathing, he thought about all he had waiting back home— his job, his brothers, his life.

He knew already, even after just ten days with Sofie, that she was forever tied to this place. The desert around Albuquerque, the mountains, the canyons and the mesas, they were part of her, part of the blood pulsing through her veins. Taking her away from her family wasn't an option.

He would have to be the one to give up everything he knew. Cameron drew a deep breath. But there were no sailboats in the desert. And he didn't know much else.

Drawing a ragged breath, he closed his eyes. He had a lot more to work out before he and Sofie had a happily-ever-after. But he'd think about all of that tomorrow.

Sofie left Cameron before the sun rose. He was still asleep in her bed, his long limbs tangled in the pale blue sheets, his face pressed into one of her pillows. She knew if she woke him he'd want to come with her, but this was something she needed to do on her own.

She drove west, away from the rising sun, toward Vulture Creek. The air was cool and the sky clear. Sofie smiled to herself as she replayed the events of the previous night and her pulse quickened. She couldn't remember the last time she'd felt so completely alive, as if the future was just waiting for her to reach out and grab it.

She'd spent far too long regretting past mistakes, trying to recapture something that she thought she'd lost. She was tired of looking back. Maybe she'd never be a cop again. Maybe the accident had changed the course of her life. But now she was beginning to see the possibilities that lay in front of her.

Sofie laughed. A few months ago, she'd been entirely focused on her career, determined to get back onto the force and regain her position in the department. And yet here she was, actually imagining herself married—and sometimes there were even children in the picture.

Though she'd always assumed she'd settle down someday, once she'd started work, that option had been pushed into the shadows. The subject of marriage had never come up between her and Sam, mostly because she usually left the room if it sounded as if the discussion was heading in that direction.

But now her future was no longer carved in stone. She could make it whatever she chose. And if she chose to spend it with Cameron, then so many wonderful things were possible.

As she drove, she thought about all the things they could share, all the adventures they could have together. She was so engrossed in her thoughts that she nearly missed the entrance to the ranch.

She'd driven past the place a number of times and studied an aerial view on Google Maps. But this time, Sofie had a reason to open the gate and drive to the ranch house. She had business with the owner.

The place looked nothing like the typical ranch houses in the area, weathered by the wind. The log house gleamed in the morning light, its multipaned windows reflecting the sun and its wide porch shading the front door.

When she stopped the Jeep, Sofie took a moment to gather her thoughts before walking up the front steps. She had no idea if this would work, but she had to give it a try. She took the steps two at a time and then rang the front bell.

A few seconds later the door swung open and Vivian Armstrong appeared. A smile broke across her face, followed very quickly by a look of confusion. "Sofie. What are you doing here? How did you—"

"Can I come in? We need to talk."

"I—I don't know. Walter isn't here and he doesn't like it if—"

"Vivian, it's important. Believe me."

She clutched the edge of the door, and Sofie was sure she was about to slam it shut. But then she finally stepped back and motioned for Sofie to enter. "Why are you here? I thought you went back to San Francisco. When I called you for our mud bath, they said you'd checked out."

"I live in Albuquerque, not San Francisco, Vivian. And I'm a private investigator. Your sister, Stella, hired me to find out if her husband was cheating on her."

The color drained out of Vivian's face. "Stella knows about me?"

"Not yet. She suspects there's a woman, but she has no idea it's you."

"Pictures," Vivian murmured. "You took pictures

of us. You pretended to be my friend." She turned away, hurrying across the room to stand near a huge stone fireplace. Vivian rubbed her arms, as if she was cold—or afraid. "And Cameron?"

"He was working with me."

"Oh." The word came out as more of a groan than an exclamation of understanding. "Oh, no. I—I think you should probably leave." Vivian pointed to the door with a shaky hand.

"I'm not going to leave until we talk." Sofie's heart twisted at the stricken expression on Vivian's face.

"What do we have to talk about? You're going to tell Stella about me. And then she'll hate me forever."

"I took the photos, but I'm not going to give them to Stella."

Vivian's eyes filled with tears and her voice wavered with emotion. "You—you aren't?"

"You need to talk to her yourself. You need to tell her what's going on and how you feel. You'll never be able to keep this a secret forever."

"I don't want to hurt my sister."

"Then you shouldn't have started sleeping with her husband."

Vivian burst into tears, covering her face with her hands as she sobbed. Sofie crossed the room and slipped her arm around Vivian's shoulders, guiding her over to the leather sofa. They both sat down, and Sofie gently patted Vivian's back, hoping that her crying would be soothed.

"This is a disaster," Vivian said.

"It is," Sofie agreed. "It's a real mess."

"She's going to hate me."

"Maybe she will. But didn't you know that when you started seeing Walter?"

"Walter's political career will be ruined. He can't take a scandal like this. And——and he'll lose everything in the divorce."

"Not everything," Sofie said. "You'll still have this ranch."

Vivian glanced up. "Not just that. We still have our collection. Walter said we're keeping it for a rainy day."

"Your collection?"

"It's in the library. He says it's worth a lot. He's invested my money in it, and he's assured me it's better than stocks and bonds. Stella doesn't know anything about it, so she shouldn't be able to touch it."

Sofie slowly stood. She pointed to a set of French doors. "This way?"

Vivian nodded. "Just don't touch anything. He's really fussy. Some of the pieces are really valuable."

Sofie walked through the doors to the library, then froze, a tiny gasp slipping from her lips. The floor-to-ceiling wooden shelves had been cleared of books and were now lined with Native American artifacts. She moved closer, her gaze taking in the massive collection. There had to be at least a couple million dollars in looted pieces, beautiful bowls and urns, ladles without a single crack or chip. But as she got closer, she began to see that something wasn't quite right.

Though the artifacts looked old and the patina was almost perfect, Sofie could tell they were fakes. She'd seen plenty of the real thing in her mother's gallery and in museums.

Her mother was one of New Mexico's foremost experts in authenticating legally collected artifacts. Talie Reyes had no patience for anything collected illegally. But was this illegal, to dupe a man intent on breaking the law?

She picked up a pot and turned it over. The even color of the patina was a dead giveaway. And a tiny chip in the side revealed the real color of the clay. The oils from handling the pot over a hundred years would have sunk deeply into the clay, not just sit on the surface.

"Please don't touch those," Vivian said.

Sofie turned, the pot still clutched in her hands. "How much of your money has he invested, Vivian?"

"I don't know. Maybe a quarter million. I have an inheritance from my father."

Sofie drew a deep breath. "Vivian, these are fakes. They're modern pots made to look old. This one here," she said, pointing to a bowl on the middle shelf, "I think this actually might be one of my mother's bowls. She's a potter in Albuquerque and sells these to tourists for a hundred dollars."

"No. Walter says they're an investment. He gets them right from the people who dig them up."

"The people out at the dig site near the airstrip?"

Vivian nodded. "Yes."

"If you don't believe me, you can take them to my mother's gallery and have them authenticated, but I'm pretty sure you've been swindled. What I'm not sure of, however, is whether Walter is doing the swindling or if he's been duped, as well."

"What do you mean?"

Sofie crossed the room and took Vivian's hand. "He took money from you, and he gave you these things that are worth nothing. Maybe he bought them cheap and kept some of the money for himself?"

Vivian's eyes filled with sudden tears. "No. No, he wouldn't do that. Walter thinks they're real. They are real."

Reaching for an arrowhead, Sofie held it out. "This looks real. Maybe there are a few pieces in here that are authentic. I'd guess they were the first things that the perps sold Walter, in case he had them checked out. But after they'd lured him in, they sold him the big-ticket items. And those have been made to look old." Sofie paused. "They probably told him these treasures came off government land, which would make them illegal to possess. But there's a huge black market for artifacts. That's where the money is. Don't you see, Vivian? Either way, it doesn't make Walter look like a good guy."

"You—you need to go. You need to go right now," Vivian said. "I don't want you here anymore."

Sofie crossed to the desk and scribbled her cell-phone number on a scrap of paper, then returned to Vivian. She pressed the paper into her hand. "I'm not going to give the photos to Stella. But you need to think about yourself here." She met Vivian's wide-eyed gaze. "If you need my help, just give me a call."

Vivian drew a ragged breath. "He loves me," she said.

"I really do hope that's true, Vivian."

With that, Sofie decided that she'd done all she could. As she stepped out onto the wide porch, she realized that her attempt to clean up a mess just made things a lot messier. Poor Vivian. If she'd been swindled by Walter, the betrayal would be almost too much to bear. And if Walter had been unaware of the pottery's origins, then he wasn't nearly as smart as Sofie had given him credit for.

An idea teased at her thoughts, and as she started the Jeep, she realized there was a way to discover the truth. Now that she knew about Walter's marital infidelities, she would start investigating his newfound hobby. Someone out at the dig site was involved in this, either providing Walter with fake pottery or raking in a lot of cash duping collectors who'd be too afraid to get the items authenticated.

Cameron hadn't started the kitchen remodel at Carlo's house yet. Maybe they could fit this in first. She smiled to herself. She had an excuse to keep him all to herself just a little bit longer.

"One last case," Sofie said. "And then I'll be ready to let him go."

8

CAMERON HAD NEVER seen the desert looking more beautiful. And he could say the same for his companion, the exotic creature sitting in the passenger seat of the Jeep.

She was dressed in faded jeans and a tank top, her straw cowboy hat pulled down against the late-afternoon sun. She'd pulled off her cowboy boots and had kicked her bare feet up on the edge of the door, her red-painted toenails shining in the sun.

Cameron smiled to himself. There were moments spent with Sofie when he believed his life couldn't get any better. He'd become completely infatuated with her in the course of just a few weeks. How would he feel in another three weeks? Somehow, it was hard to believe that this contentment would ever fade.

Three weeks seemed like an eternity, but if the hours passed as quickly as the first three weeks had, then he didn't have much time left at all. Cameron knew the connection they'd found was rare. It was as if they'd been created for each other, put into the world to be together.

They'd been staying at Sofie's apartment in Albuquerque, but today, Sofie had decided they needed to get out of town. She'd packed the tent and sleeping bags, along with a cooler full of food and drinks, then told him to drive west, chasing the sun across the sky.

"Where are we going?" he asked.

"We're going to do a favor for a friend," she said.

"I don't have any friends around here, except for you," he said.

"Actually, this is a friend of my mother's."

"I like your mom," Cameron said.

Sofie turned and smiled. "And she likes you. But then, she likes everyone. My father says that if it weren't for her, he wouldn't have any friends."

"How did they meet?"

"My mom was in college in Santa Fe and Dad had just taken a job with the police department there. She was working in an art gallery, and he was on foot patrol. He walked by and saw her through the window. She smiled at him and that was it. He came back the next day with lunch and kept stopping by every day until she agreed to go out with him. He says he fell in love with her the moment she smiled at him."

"Do you think it's possible?" Cameron asked.

"What?"

"Love at first sight?"

Her brow furrowed as she considered the question for a long moment. "I'm not sure. I suppose it depends if those feelings last. If they do, then it was love at first sight. If they don't, then it was just lust at first sight."

"Good point," he said. He reached out and rested his hand on the back of her seat, his finger tangling in the hair at her nape. "I think if you believe in love at first sight, you have to believe in destiny, too. The idea that two people are meant to find each other, against all odds."

"All dreams spin out from the same web," Sofie said. She laughed. "That's another one of my mother's sayings."

"What does it mean?"

"I think it means that everyone's dreams are interconnected in some way. That your dream to become a paleontologist caused your grandfather to send you to Vulture Creek, where I met you, and you helped me with the case, which is helping me make a living while I work toward getting back on the force, which is my dream." She giggled softly. "At least that's what I think it means. Sometimes my mother's Hopi wisdom can be a bit mystifying."

"All dreams come from the same web?" Cameron asked.

"All dreams spin out from the same web," Sofie corrected.

As they drove through the desert, Cameron thought about the words. He'd never really had any dreams as an adult. From the moment his parents had disappeared, he'd taken on responsibility for his brothers, for keeping the family solid. And his efforts had been a success. He and his brothers were best friends. And it had been enough—until now.

Cameron had always known he ought to want more. While men his age were getting married and having children, he was still wasting time with short-term affairs. He was satisfying his physical needs with no-strings sex and ignoring whatever emotional needs he might have.

He'd been treading water, waiting for a lifeboat to drift by and throw him a line. And now here was the line, floating right in front of him, and he was afraid to grab hold. Could he convince Sofie that they belonged together?

Her skeptical nature didn't say much for his odds, but he had to try anyway. But Cameron wasn't sure what he was supposed to say. Relationships were supposed to grow slowly, so each person had time to decide what they wanted. Cameron felt as if everything between him and Sofie had been accelerated from the start.

He still had another three weeks left, but hell, he didn't know what they were doing tomorrow, much less a week or two from now. He had to take his chances while he could.

They headed off the road, the Jeep bouncing through rough terrain before Sofie pointed to a distant outcropping. "Right over there," she said.

As they drove closer, Cameron saw a pair of ATVs parked near a stone fire ring. A couple of teenage boys waved as they approached, then hopped on the ATVs and drove off. Cameron turned to Sofie. "Do you know them?"

She shook her head. "Nope."

"What are we doing here?"

"We're going to camp. And we're also going to guard this site from looters."

"Looters?"

Sofie nodded. "The man who owns this land has agreed to give up any artifacts found to the Museum of Indian Arts and Culture in Santa Fe. But looters have been sneaking onto the property and digging in the site. So, my mother and some of her friends on the museum board have set up a schedule for people to come out here and guard the site until the museum can get to it."

"What are we going to do if we see any looters?" he asked. "Throw rocks at them?"

Sofie shook her head. "I have my gun in the Jeep."

"You have a gun?"

"Don't look so surprised. I'm a cop. I have several guns."

He grinned at her. "I've never been with a woman who was armed," he said.

She leaned over and brushed a kiss across his lips. "If you talk sweet to me, I'll teach you how to shoot." She slid out of the truck and began to unload supplies from the back. He grabbed the tent from her and carried it over to a flat spot near the fire pit. Chopped wood was already stacked neatly nearby, and someone had brought a big barrel of water for washing dishes.

"This is nice," he said.

Sofie took the tent bag from his hands and dropped it on the dusty ground. "Come on, let me show you what we're protecting."

He laced his fingers through hers and walked along beside her to the base of a jagged outcropping. Cameron could see that the rock and earth had been crumbling beneath the elements. She hitched her hands on her hips as she stared out at the site.

"There's a Hopi proverb that says if we dig precious things from the land, we invite disaster."

Sofie bent down and picked up what looked like a jagged rock. But when she turned it over, he saw a design on the back. "This was probably a ceremonial bowl," she said, placing the shard back where she found it. She pointed to another spot and held up a small sliver of rock. "This was likely used as a tool, to cut or scrape. You can see how the edge has been flaked to make it sharp."

"So what's to stop you from putting those things in your pocket?"

"Nothing. There are no security cameras or armed guards. That's why it's so frustrating. The thieves go after a place like this like vultures. Then, once they dig the artifacts out of the ground, it's all about the money." She pointed to a shard embedded in a clump of dirt. "Once the site is known, it's an open invitation to looters." She pointed to freshly exposed soil. "You can see where they dug right here. Most of the looting happens on public or tribal land. Even though digging there is illegal, there are lots of artifacts to be found and very few rangers to watch over it all. But at least these things will be saved before they hit the black market."

"I'm glad you brought me out here."

"There's another reason," she said. "I went to see Vivian a few days ago."

"At the ranch?" he asked.

"I wanted to talk to her alone, to try to convince her to talk to Stella herself. Then I found out what Walter was doing out at the dig site." She scrapped the dry soil with her boot. "He's been taking Vivian's money and buying what he thinks are smuggled artifacts. He has quite a collection. According to Vivian, he's spent close to a quarter of a million dollars of her money on them."

"And you think they're looted?"

She shook her head. "No. I know they're not looted. At least the good stuff isn't. They're fakes."

"Why would someone sell fakes?"

"There's a huge black market for artifacts. And if the buyer knows they're smuggled, they don't dare get anything authenticated. So the seller takes no risk in looting and gets all the reward from customers with money to burn. It's a perfect setup, a lot like the fake sports-memorabilia market, especially if you can find a naive collector."

"So the guy is duped, never learning that he's bought fakes—"

"Unless he tries to sell them to another collector. Only then will he find out that he's been swindled. Bu by that point, the sellers are long gone."

"Now that you know what he was doing at the dig site, are you going to give Stella the photos?"

"I don't think it's as easy as that," Sofie said. "Here's a guy who cheats on his wife. He takes her money and spends it on his mistress. And then, he takes his mistress's money and invests in black-market artifacts. I think Walter knows they're fake and he's using the purchases to steal money from Vivian. I'd be willing to bet that he's paid about ten thousand for all he's bought and pocketed the rest of Vivian's money. That's what he's using to finance his real-estate investments.

Cameron ran his hand through his hair, shaking his head. "What a mess," he murmured.

She grabbed his hand. "I was thinking, maybe we could work another case together. We could see if we can find the people selling the fake artifacts and try to get Vivian's money back for her."

"You think they'll just give it back?"

"Well, we could threaten to go to the FBI unless they do. That might make them agree to cut their losses."

"Why all this concern for Vivian?"

"I don't know. I mean, I'd never let myself trust a man like Walter. He's already cheated. But still, she loves him. I'm not sure she even knows the real Walter, but she's just put her heart out there and is ready to believe. I kind of admire that." Sofie sighed. "If Walter really is a creep, then he's going to leave her a quarter of a million dollars poorer. She might never be able to trust a man again."

"I think we make a pretty good team," he said. "If anyone can get her money back, we can."

Sofie pushed up on her toes and threw her arms around his neck. "We are a good team," she said. "I'm the brains behind the operation and you're the beauty."

He growled softly, pressing a kiss against her neck. "I think you're both the brains and the beauty. I'm just your assistant."

"Yes, but you're awfully pretty, too." She pulled him along toward the campsite. "Come on, let's get settled and then I'll let you make me dinner. After that, I might take you inside my tent and have my way with you."

Cameron followed along after her. "Can we do that tent thing first? 'Cause I'm really not that hungry."

SOFIE WASN'T SURE what woke her up. But she sat up, feeling around in the dark interior of the tent for Cameron. To her surprise, his sleeping bag was gone and so was he.

Grabbing her own sleeping bag and wrapping it around her naked body, Sofie crawled out of the tent. The night air was cold on her skin, and she shivered as she scanned the campsite for Cameron.

She saw him sitting just beyond the fire, his body outlined by the light from the moon, his face tipped up to the sky. He'd wrapped himself up and was sitting cross-legged on the ground.

"What are you doing out here?" she asked. "It's freezing."

"Come here," he said.

She walked across the hard-packed ground around the fire. He stood and wrapped his sleeping bag around them both. "Did you hear something?" Sofie asked. "You should have woken me."

"No, there was nothing. I just woke up and came out to look at the stars and then—"

"What?" Sofie asked.

"It sounds silly."

"You heard voices," she said.

Cameron gasped. "I did. I was just sitting by the fire and I started hearing things. Like whispers. But I didn't understand the words."

She nodded. "Yeah, that happens. I used to think it was the spirit world talking to me."

"Is it?"

Sofie shrugged. "If you believe in the spirit world, yes. If you don't, I guess it's just your ears playing tricks on you. It's leftover sounds from your day, still vibrating in your head. It's the wind or the animals or echoes from a nearby town."

"Why would the spirit world be talking to a guy like me? I'm Irish."

"I don't know," she said, turning her face up to his. "You have to figure that out on your own."

His hands smoothed over her hips, then moved to her backside, pulling her against him as he kissed her. Sofie sighed as the kiss grew more passionate. He was all she ever needed. How had she gone so long without this? When Cameron touched her, every atom in her body came alive. She felt as if nature had created them for each other.

But it wasn't just the physical attraction that she'd come to need. There was an emotional connection between the two of them, a trust that she'd never had with a man before. She could say anything to him, reveal her deepest secrets, and Sofie knew that he'd accept her for exactly who she was.

There were moments when she wanted to open her heart, to admit that she was falling in love with him, just to see his reaction. Was he feeling the same way? Sofie knew it was too soon to talk about the future, but she'd never been one to hide her feelings.

"Do you remember the other night when I said that you were my boyfriend?"

"I do," Cameron said.

"It wasn't just to prove a point to my father or my relatives. I just wanted to— I needed you to know that—"

"Tell me," he said.

"I think this is a good thing, you and me. I think we're good together. And I think I should stop talking before I ruin everything." She cleared her throat. "I just wanted you to know that."

"I understand exactly how you feel," Cameron said. "When I first kissed you, I thought, this will be fun. A good way to pass my time while I'm in New Mexico. But somewhere along the line, it turned into a lot more than just fun."

"See," she cried. "You're so good at saying these things, and I can barely put a sentence together."

"Try again," he said.

Sofie shook her head. "I'll just mess it up. I'm better at showing you." She ran her hand down his chest, trailing kisses after her touch.

"Tell me," he said, rubbing her upper arms.

She drew a shaky breath. "I'm very— I'm growing very fond of you. And I think it's important that you know."

"Why?" Cameron asked.

"Because I have to say it out loud. It's important, and if I don't say it, it won't be real. It won't feel real. And out here, with the spirits listening, I need to tell the truth."

He pulled her into a long, passionate kiss. Sofie knew his feelings were just as intense and overwhelming as hers. "I think you better come back inside before you catch a cold," she said.

"I'm going to stay out here a little longer," he said.

"Not too long, okay?" she said. Pushing up on her toes, she gave him a kiss, then left him standing by the fire.

She unzipped the tent and crawled back inside, laying out her sleeping bag again on the tent floor. When she was curled up inside the down cocoon, Sofie closed her eyes. It was easy to forget the real world existed when she was out in the desert. Everything was at its simplest, its most elemental. She could think; her mind was clear.

Sofie had almost drifted off to sleep when Cameron crawled back into the tent, snuggling up next to her. "I'm freezing," he whispered.

"That's what you get for running around half-naked in the desert."

"Warm me up."

With a dramatic sigh, Sofie raised the edge of her sleeping bag and Cameron slid over, wrapping his arms around her waist and pulling her warm body against his. The sensations racing through her had become familiar, but no less exciting. She knew exactly what would happen between them, and she wanted him moving inside her, bringing her to a shattering release.

"Did you solve all the world's problems out there?" she asked.

"No. Not even close. But I figured a few things out."

"Like what?" she whispered, her lips soft against his.

"Like what I need to say to you."

Sofie felt butterflies in her stomach, and for a moment, she forgot to breathe. Had she made a mistake earlier? Had she revealed too much, too soon? "And what is that?"

"I know some people don't take these words seriously, but I want you to know that I've never said this before. And I may never say it again. And I'm not really sure whether I should be saying it now, but here goes. I'm pretty sure that I'm falling in love with you."

"Pretty sure?" she asked.

"I've never felt like this before, Sofie. But it seems like that's what's happening here."

"You figured all this out while you were listening to the voices?" she asked.

"While I was out there, I was so cold. And all I could think about was you, safe and warm inside the tent. And I realized I didn't want to warm up with anyone else but you." He reached up and touched her face. "We don't have to figure anything out right now, Sofie. But my feelings aren't going to change. In another few weeks, we're going to have to make some tough choices. I just want you to think about that."

"I have been thinking about it," Sofie said. "I didn't expect to fall in love with you, either. But that's the only explanation I have for how I feel when I'm with you. We've been together for such a short time, but I can't imagine spending a night without you."

"Then promise me we won't."

"I'm not sure we can make those kinds of promises," Sofie said. "I'm not sure we can make *any* promises."

"It's going to work out," Cameron said. "It has to."

Sofie kissed him again, then pulled him on top of her. He was hard and ready, and all she wanted was to feel that perfect intimacy between them. She moved against him, and for a moment, he was inside her.

He reached out for the box of condoms he'd packed, but Sofie grabbed his hand. "We don't need those," she said.

"We don't?"

"I've had that covered all along."

"Yes?" he asked.

She nodded. "So maybe we can just…"

"You're sure?"

"I am," she whispered.

He slowly buried himself deep inside her, and Sofie closed her eyes as a maelstrom of exquisite sensation raced through her body. It was different now, she mused. They were together, and there was no need to hold anything back.

THE TANTALIZING SCENTS of breakfast drifted out into the morning air as Cameron opened the door to Millie's diner. After a night spent in carnal pleasures in the middle of the desert, he was ravenous and was already thinking about what he'd order for breakfast.

Sofie had dropped him off and was waiting in the Jeep for a few minutes before she came inside to observe. She'd spent the ride into Vulture Creek reviewing what he was supposed to do, and Cameron felt confident that he could charm his way onto the dig site. After all, how could they refuse a strong back and a winning personality?

He nodded at Millie as he walked inside, then sat down at the counter.

"You're back," Millie said. "Where's your partner in crime?"

"She'll be in in a few minutes. Listen, we're not supposed to know each other. Don't let on, okay?"

Millie nodded quickly. "You ready to order?" she asked, changing the subject.

"You bet." Cameron proceeded to order a Denver omelet, hash browns and orange juice. Millie poured him a cup of coffee, then walked away to place the order with the cook.

The group from the dig was gathered around their usual table, still waiting for their breakfast. Cameron watched them in the reflection of the mirror behind the counter. The group was a mix of twenty-something grad students and what looked like re-tirees.

He took a quick sip of his coffee, drew a deep breath and pushed to his feet. They didn't notice him until he was standing next to the table. "Hey, there," he said, shoving his hands in his jeans pockets. "I don't mean to interrupt, but Millie was telling me that you're digging for dinosaur bones around here. She said you might be looking for some volunteers."

A young man with wire-rimmed glasses and a beard glanced up at him. "You ever worked on a dig site?" he asked.

"No. But I've been fascinated by paleontology since I was a kid. And I'm not afraid of hard work. It would be cool to experience what a real dig is like."

"Oh, give him a chance, Ron," an elderly woman said. "Florence and I will watch over him, won't we, Flo?" She turned to her left and smiled at another elderly woman, almost an exact replica of herself. "I'm Gertrude and this is my sister, Florence. We're the Winegarten sisters. We do this every summer."

"We're finishing up this phase of the dig," Ron said. "We've only got a few days before we pack up and head back home, so you might not see a big discovery. But we could use your help breaking camp."

"When can I start?" Cameron asked.

"You could ride out with us," Gertrude said. "We have room in our car."

"Yes," Flo said. "Ride with us."

Cameron nodded. "All right."

The bell above the door jangled, and he glanced over to see Sofie walk in. A few of the young men at the table watched as she slid into a spot at the far end of the counter.

"She's back," one of the male students whispered.

"Maybe she was on vacation," a girl said. "Why don't you go introduce yourself?"

"A woman like that scares me. She's almost too beautiful."

"Pity about that limp," the girl said. "My great-aunt has a limp. From polio."

Cameron fought the urge to jump to Sofie's defense. Not a single person at the table knew what an extraordinary person she was. Not one realized that they were lucky to be caught inside her orbit. Yes, she was beautiful, but she was so much more.

A moment later, Millie arrived at the table with a huge tray of breakfast plates. "Will you take your breakfast at the counter or should I bring it to the table?" she asked.

"Sit here!" Gertrude said, patting an empty seat next to her.

Once the seating arrangements were made, the students in the group dug into their meals, and the Winegarten sisters began their interrogation. Cameron decided to stick with the facts. The only part of his story that changed was his reason for being in Vulture Creek. He told the group that he'd come looking for a warm-weather vacation home.

Every now and then, he'd catch Sofie's eye, and he kept hoping that she'd wander over and volunteer, as well. Together, they'd be able to figure out exactly what was going on at the dig site. Alone, Cameron was afraid he'd manage to blow it.

Right now there were twelve suspects sitting at the table. The head of the dig, a Dr. Crowley, had left the previous day to prepare for the next semester of classes. In truth, Cameron was glad he wouldn't have to bear the scrutiny of the big boss.

"Florence and I just love spending our summers digging," Gert said. "It's so exciting to be a part of all this."

"What do you do in the winter months?" Cameron asked.

"Oh, we travel. Europe, Asia. Last summer we took a monthlong safari to Africa. Kenya. It was lovely."

"And what did you do before you retired?" he asked.

"We were schoolteachers," Florence said. "I taught history and Gertie taught art. We never married. We were always so devoted to our students."

Cameron made a mental note to investigate the pair more closely. He didn't know many schoolteachers who could afford lavish trips on their retirement income.

As he chatted with the rest of the dig's volunteers and paid employees, he found a few more suspects. Though Ron seemed like a by-the-book kind of guy, his friend Sebastian set off all kinds of alarm bells in Cameron's mind. He seemed nervous talking about himself, as if he was afraid he might not remember the right lies. And he kept glancing at the door, which was another red flag.

Fred was another retiree, an ex-fireman from Prescott, Arizona. Cameron sensed that he'd never besmirch his reputation with a forgery scam. The rest of the members didn't give off any signals that made him suspicious, although Sofie had warned him that the most successful scam artists were those who rarely stood out.

He did take a second look at Mrs. Betty Tompkins, Professor Crowley's executive assistant and the second in command behind Ron. When Cameron tried to engage her, she coldly cut him off.

Breakfast was over before he knew it, and Cameron gulped down the last of his coffee before tossing down some cash for the check. He sent one last glance Sofie's way as he walked to the door and she nodded.

The ride out to the dig site took just over fifteen minutes. The Winegarten sisters traveled in style in a tricked-out Escalade with an expensive sound system and leather seats.

"This is a nice ride," he commented.

Gert smiled. "We had a Lexus, but Florence insisted on buying American this time around."

"Teaching must have been good to you."

"Oh, we've always been thrifty," Gert explained. "Two single girls don't have much to do with their money but save it. And we've made some rather lucrative investments. Of course, Florence got us into computer technology when Intel was a steal."

"IBM, too," Florence said.

"And now we have enough money to enjoy our retirement. You mentioned that you worked for your family's business. What is that, dear?" Gert asked.

"We build luxury sailing yachts."

"Oh, yachts," Gert said. "My, that must be interesting."

"It pays the bills," Cameron said.

The subject changed back to the travels of the Winegarten sisters, and Cameron let his thoughts wander as they described their visit to the Great Wall of China. Though he'd been surprised by Sofie's plan to help Vivian, he had to wonder if their own romantic relationship had made her more sensitive to Vivian's dilemma.

Someday, he'd get to the bottom of Sofie's trust issues. He suspected there was more to her breakup with Sam than his reaction to her accident. He could only imagine how an incident like Sofie's could affect a relationship, even one that was solid in the first place.

If he'd known Sofie back then, he'd have done everything he could to dissuade her from going back to the police force. Sure, it was her dream, but dreams could change. He'd learned that here in New Mexico.

The Escalade pulled to a stop, and Cameron looked out the window. This had been his dream a long time ago. And now, as he stared at the tents and the crates and the equipment scattered about, Cameron realized that there was nothing here that he really needed.

"Come along," Flo said. "We'll show you the ropes before Ron has a chance to put you on outhouse duty."

"He's going to make me clean the outhouse?" Cameron asked.

"You're low man on the roster," Gert said. "But if we request your help, he'll find someone else. Flo, get out your medicine. You'll need to have another one of your spells."

Cameron chuckled. He sure hoped the Winegarten sisters weren't scam artists. He was beginning to like them.

"Lead the way," he said, offering them both an arm.

9

SOFIE WATCHED THE Winegarten sisters hurry out of the hotel bar, the two ladies anxious to escape any further questioning. "They would have been the last people I suspected," Sofie said.

"It's ingenious," Cameron said. "They buy reproductions and dirty them up a little, then warn the customers not to sell them for at least five years. They know how to spot an easy mark a mile away."

"What tipped you off?"

"They just seemed too wealthy to have been schoolteachers. And they have a terrible weakness for handsome young men. I just started flirting with them, and they seemed so eager to please. When I mentioned my arrowhead collection, they just couldn't resist showing me theirs."

"They are a lot smarter than they look," Sofie said. "Which makes them the perfect pair to pull this off. I have to wonder if the schoolteacher story is even true."

Cameron shrugged. "Does it really matter?" he said, holding out the cashier's check. "We got Vivian's money back."

"Do you think we can believe them on the amount?"

"I don't think they were in any position to lie to us," Cameron said.

"I couldn't have done this without your help," Sofie said.

"We make a good team."

In truth, they made the best team. When they were together, everything clicked. He'd given her the confidence to trust again—to trust herself and to trust in love.

Cameron hadn't tried to change her; he'd simply stood back and loved the person she was, beneath the fears and insecurities. She'd gone so long believing that she was flawed, that the scar on her hip had gone as deep as her soul. But he'd taught her that her accident didn't define her anymore.

"You know what this means," Sofie murmured.

"There's still a hundred and fifty thousand of Vivian's money missing," he replied.

The sisters had kept meticulous records. As a condition for Sofie's silence, the Winegartens had been required to photocopy the book and leave the copy with Sofie.

After reading the records that involved Walter, Sofie was certain that everything in the library was provided by the Winegarten sisters. The man had been buying from them for three summers, snatching up almost everything they had to offer.

"Maybe he's squirreled it away in a safe place, just for a rainy day," he said. "Is this our next case? Finding out where the money is? We could get it back."

Sofie shook her head. "No, Walter and Vivian are going to have to work this out on their own." She glanced over her shoulder to the door. "You know, what we just did could technically be considered extortion. They could call the police."

Cameron took the cashier's check from her fingers and examined it. "We asked them to do the right thing. To return money they'd stolen. And then we informed them of the consequences if they didn't comply. They made the right decision."

"Some might say we threatened them," Sofie said.

"I don't think the Winegarten sisters will be filing a complaint with the authorities anytime soon."

"Do you think they'll stop swindling would-be collectors?"

"I don't know. I think they were genuinely frightened. And I'd guess they're upstairs packing right now, hoping to get as far away from us as possible. They'll probably keep scamming, but maybe they'll choose something other than Native American artifacts."

"At least their business was keeping the buyers away from the real stuff." She smiled. "I think we should celebrate another case solved. All that's left is to take the check the Vivian and see what Walter has to say for himself." Sofie waved the cocktail waitress over to their table. "We'd like a bottle of champagne," she said.

"Actually, cancel that order," Cameron said. He stood up and held out his hand. "Let's get out of here. We can find a much better spot to celebrate."

"I think I have a bottle of champagne at home," she said. "It's about six years old, but it should still be good."

"You haven't had anything to celebrate in six years?" Cameron asked.

"Not that I can recall," she said, folding the check in half and putting it in her pocket. "I think I was going to drink it for New Year's Eve once, but then I fell asleep."

He tucked her hand into his as they walked out into the lobby. "I can promise you, your New Year's Eves are going to get a lot better from now on."

"And why is that?"

"Because you're going to spend them with me," Cameron said. "When are you going to give the check to Vivian?"

"I thought I'd drive it out there tomorrow."

"Can I come with you?"

Sofie shook her head. "I think it would be best if I go alone. If Walter is there, things could get messy. And I don't need you to make them messier."

"What's that supposed to mean?"

"Walter would not be happy to see you. He might

yell at me, but he could punch you. He's known to have a pretty bad temper."

"I really think I should come along, Sof," Cameron said. "What if the situation becomes something you can't—"

"I know what I'm doing," Sofie snapped. There was a sharp edge to her voice that she hadn't heard for a long time and she felt suddenly defensive. "I'm sorry," she said.

"No, it's all right," he muttered. "Hey, I'm just your employee. I'm not supposed to offer an opinion."

"You know that's not how I feel. It was just an instinctive reaction. Sam used to tell me what to do all the time. So did my father and my brothers. They were always worried that I couldn't handle myself."

"I know you can handle yourself," Cameron said. "I trust you. It's the other guy I have a problem with."

"Well, you're going to have to get used to it if I go back to police work," she said.

Sofie wasn't sure what made her say the words. She'd already decided that it was best to move forward, to find another dream for herself. Yet she wanted to see his reaction, to see how much control he intended to exert on her life.

He stared at her for a long moment. "I thought you were moving on," he said.

Sofie shook her head. "I haven't made any decisions about my future. My hip is feeling better every day. I could be ready to go back next year."

She wanted to stop, but something drove her on. Was she trying to sabotage the relationship by forcing him into a corner? Or were her fears about commitment finally bubbling to the surface?

"I'm not like Sam," Cameron said. "And I'm certainly not like Walter. You need to decide what you want, Sofie. For yourself, first, and then for us."

"Shouldn't those be the same thing?" she asked.

"No," he replied. "They might be completely different. I'm not going to tell you what to do. Your happiness begins with you."

"And what about you?" Sofie asked.

"I know what I need for a happy ending."

"And what is that?"

"I've decided I'm not going to go back to Seattle when my six weeks are up. I'm going to stay here, in Albuquerque."

Sofie gasped. "What?"

"I'm not going to live with you. At least not unless you want me to. But, after the six weeks, I can use my bank account again. I'm going to sell my house in Seattle and buy something down here."

"And what if I don't want that?"

"I'm willing to wait around until you figure everything out. I'm a very patient man, Sofie."

"You can't give up your job. How are you going to build sailboats here?"

"I've figured that out, too, believe it or not. I can live and work here and fly to Seattle once a week for meetings. I make a really good living. And I think, since my grandfather was the one who insisted on this trip, he isn't allowed to be disappointed at my decision."

Sofie opened her mouth to speak, but she couldn't put her feelings into words. She was shocked. And uneasy. He had this all figured out, after just three weeks together. Cameron knew exactly what he needed, and he had a plan to make it happen. She, on the other hand, was still trying to adjust to the notion that she might finally be in love.

"That's a very big decision to make after such a short time," Sofie said.

"I know what I want."

"You think you know," Sofie said. "But maybe you don't. And maybe I don't. I'm just saying we should take some time before we make any rash—"

"Rash? You think this is rash?"

"No. I meant…quick. Or important."

"Those two things don't have the same meaning. Say what you mean, Sofie. Tell me the truth."

"I don't know what the truth is," Sofie said, walking toward the Jeep. "Why do we have to plan this out so soon? Can't we just wait and see where things lead us? Maybe then we could make a decision based on reality, instead of some fantasy."

"What fantasy?" he shouted.

"This fantasy that you have in your head that we can just live happily-ever-after without even knowing what we really want. Or who we really are."

"I know who I am, Sofie."

"Good for you. But maybe I don't know. Maybe I'm not sure. And forcing me to decide the rest of my life right now isn't helping one bit."

They drove home in silence, both of them lost in their own thoughts. It wasn't difficult to listen to all the negative voices in her head. She'd been dealing with disappointment for so long that it sometimes felt like the safest place to be.

Sofie knew it was holding her back, this belief that the rest of her life would be a struggle. She had every reason to be blissfully happy, to see her future with Cameron for what it was, a dream come true. He'd already given her so much. Why couldn't she just take that last little leap, that last bit of her journey that required faith rather than common sense?

When they reached her apartment, they walked inside together. Sofie ran her hands through her hair and sighed softly. She knew they ought to talk this all out, but she wasn't sure that an argument or a discussion would change anything between them. "I'm going to go to bed now. I'm tired and cranky. And I don't have anything more to say." Sofie paused. "Are you coming?"

Cameron shook his head as he flopped down on the sofa. "No. Not right now. Maybe later."

Sofie left him sitting in the living room, staring at the blank screen of the television. When she got to the bedroom, she closed the door, then crawled into bed, still dressed.

All of this had grown so complicated in such a

short time. She'd always been able to control her emotions, and now she felt as if she was riding some crazy roller coaster, bouncing between thrills and terror.

She wanted Cameron more than she'd ever wanted a man. But she'd been in charge of her own life for a long time. Sofie wasn't sure she could accept that he would have a say in her decisions, just as she'd have a say in his. That's what a committed relationship required—compromise.

What if he gave up his life in Seattle and she couldn't make him happy? Though she'd never wanted to admit it, her failure with Sam was as much her fault as his. She didn't want to make those same mistakes with Cameron.

Maybe he was right. Maybe she had to find out who she really was. Everything in her life had been shifting and changing lately. All her old beliefs had been turned upside down.

She wanted to make rational and reasonable decisions about Cameron. That was how she'd always operated. But now her emotions kept getting in the way. She'd been listening to her heart, not her head.

If only she had more time. If only she could gain a bit of perspective. Maybe then everything would be clear in her mind. Her dreams were within her reach again, only this time, they were different than before.

But Sofie couldn't bring herself to hold out her hand and grab them. Maybe she wasn't in love after all. Or maybe she was so much in love that the thought of losing Cameron was too much to bear.

Sofie turned over and buried her face in her pillow. Why did she have to figure out her future right now? She was finally learning to enjoy the present.

SHE'D PACKED A BAG in the early-morning hours, careful not to wake Cameron. Things between them had grown tense over the past few days, ever since they'd argued about his future plans.

He'd taken the job with Carlos, so he was gone for most of the day. When he came home, they both tried to pretend that everything was all right, that their disagreements would somehow work themselves out over time.

The nights were the most difficult. Sofie would go to bed early, leaving him watching sports in the living room. And then, in the middle of the night, he'd come to her and they'd make love. But instead of feeling lust and passion, sex had become almost bittersweet to her.

She felt the distance growing between them, and Sofie knew it was all her fault. She had no doubt that Cameron loved her and that he'd do anything to make their relationship work. But she couldn't bring herself to take that last step, to surrender the last piece of her heart to him.

But now she had a plan. She'd written it all out in a letter late last night. Sofie placed the note on her pillow, knowing he'd find it there when he woke up.

The decision to leave hadn't come easily, but now that she'd made it, Sofie knew that it was right.

She wasn't running away. She was searching for some space, some time to decide what she really wanted. As much as she yearned to stay with Cameron, Sofie knew that gaining any level of perspective was impossible with him living in her apartment. And she didn't have the heart to ask him to leave.

But six weeks away, six weeks to try a new life, was something that he'd understand. It was the same thing his grandfather had offered him. Sofie needed to experience the unknown. Like Cameron, she would go somewhere unfamiliar, somewhere she'd be forced to find a new job, a new home and new friends. And after six weeks, if she hadn't figured out what she wanted, then she'd probably never know.

He'd understand, she repeated to herself. And it wasn't as if this was the end for them. Hopefully, he'd be here waiting for her. And if he wasn't, she'd find him.

Sofie took one last look at the man who'd changed her life forever. She wanted to kiss him, but she knew she'd risk waking him. Instead, she gathered her resolve and walked out of the bedroom.

She had one thing to do before starting her journey. The check for Vivian was sitting on the dining-room table where they'd left it a few days before. She picked it up and tucked it in her pocket, then grabbed her keys.

As she walked to the Jeep, she thought about all

she was leaving behind. It was a risk. He might not be here when she returned. But this was something she had to do.

The sun was well over the horizon when she arrived at the ranch outside Vulture Creek. She opened the gate and drove through, then jumped out to close it behind her. As she approached the house, she noticed a single car parked out front. To her relief, it wasn't Walter's convertible.

Sofie squinted against the morning light as she climbed the front porch steps. She wasn't quite sure how this was going to go, but the fact that she was coming with a hundred thousand dollars in hand might make things a bit easier.

The sound of the doorbell filtered through the open windows of the ranch house, and she waited, wondering if Vivian might still be asleep. A few moments later, the door opened.

"Hi," Sofie said.

"What are you doing here?" Vivian murmured.

"Can I come in for a few seconds? I just have some quick business I need to take care of."

"If it's anything like the business you brought last time, then no, you can't come in. Just go away."

"It's not," Sofie said.

Vivian nodded reluctantly, then slowly opened the door. As Sofie wandered inside, she noticed the moving boxes stacked in the corner of the living room.

"What happened?"

"I told Walter I knew about his collection. He got

so angry at me—that I would think he'd steal my money, that I wouldn't trust him to have my best interests at heart. We had a huge fight. And when I asked him how much he'd spent of my money and how much he'd kept for himself, he wouldn't answer me. That's when I knew." Tears filled her eyes. "Love really sucks."

Sofie held out her arms, and Vivian crumpled into her embrace. "You'll be all right. You did the right thing."

"I've been so stupid," she continued. "And now I have nothing. No man, no money, no way to make a living."

"Did you talk to Stella?" Sofie asked.

Vivian nodded. "I told her everything. After what Walter did to me, I thought she deserved to know. She filed divorce papers a couple days ago. He's demanding spousal support. Although the prenup will probably prevent that." Vivian forced a laugh. "I guess I should have had a pre-prenup, huh?"

"You know, sometimes a fresh start can be a good thing." Sofie pulled the check from her pocket and held it out to Vivian.

"What's this?"

"Your money. Cameron and I found the people who sold Walter the artifacts. We gave them the option of refunding your money or going to prison for their activities. They chose the refund."

Vivian stared at the check in disbelief. "You got it back?"

"Not the part that Walter took. But it's enough to live on for a while. Maybe enough to stay here if you want."

She shook her head. "No. This place is just one big reminder of how stupid I was. I need to find someplace new, where no one knows me. Where I can start over."

Sofie nodded her. "I've been thinking the same thing. Where do you think you're going to go?"

"I don't know. I've always wanted to live in San Francisco. I like those trolley cars and the bridge. It looks like a really friendly place. What about you?"

"I've been thinking about Seattle," Sofie said.

"Really? Isn't that where—"

"Yeah. But I'm not going there for him," Sofie said. "I'm going there for me. To see if I can make a life for myself there."

"Good idea," Vivian said. She drew a deep breath, then shrugged. "So, I guess it's time to say goodbye." She gave Sofie a fierce hug. "Good luck, Sofie. I hope you find happiness."

"You, too, Vivian."

Sofie gave her a little wave as she walked out the front door. When she got into the Jeep, she pulled the road atlas from the backseat. Seattle. She hadn't considered that option, but now it made perfect sense. After all, Cameron had lived in her world for a while. Maybe it was time she experienced his.

Six weeks in Seattle without seeing him might be

an impossible task. But there was some comfort in the fact that he'd still be close by.

"I-25 north to Colorado," she said, reaching for the ignition. The engine rumbled. "I guess my new life has officially begun."

CAMERON STEERED his car through the late-afternoon traffic, frustrated by the constant stops and starts. He should have left the office earlier to beat the Friday-afternoon rush, but he'd been delayed when Dermot had called a last-minute production meeting.

Though he'd hoped that today would be a good one, Cameron had come to the realization that nothing was going to happen. It had been over six weeks since he'd found the note on Sofie's pillow. Six weeks and a few days since she'd walked out of his life.

He'd counted down the days, first in Albuquerque as he spent the last of his time there and now back in Seattle, back at his old job at Quinn Yachtworks. He'd expected to hear from her last week, at least in an email or a phone call to mark the six weeks she'd been gone, but there had been nothing.

He cursed softly, then reached for the car stereo and turned up the volume. It was no use thinking of her. He couldn't will her back into his life. He couldn't make her magically appear just by blinking his eyes. The only thing he could do was wait... and hope.

Cameron hadn't been the only Quinn to experience a complete reversal of his life. Strangely, all four brothers had met women, and three had gone from single to attached in those six weeks—all except for Cameron.

Dermot's girl, Rachel, was a goat farmer from Wisconsin. Kieran had found himself a country singer, Maddie West, who had arrived in Seattle a few days ago. As for Ronan, he hadn't made it home yet. He was weeks overdue, and all he would tell the family was that he might be back at Thanksgiving, Christmas at the latest.

In truth, Ronan was the only one of the brothers who'd made a truly daring decision. But then, he'd never been as tied to the business as Cameron and the twins had. He'd worked hard, but he'd never found a niche for himself, a spot where he felt comfortable.

Cameron could have stayed in New Mexico, but after his grandfather's deadline had passed, it was so much easier to make a living at his real job. He'd grown tired of sleeping in Sofie's empty bed, tired of wandering around her apartment at night, surrounded by her belongings but not her.

In the end, he got back on the bus for Seattle, determined to carry on with his life, even though it wasn't what he'd imagined for the two of them. If she wanted him, she knew where to find him.

Cameron wasn't sure how long he was willing to wait before he gave up hoping. The past few days had been sheer hell—his nights filled with thoughts of her, his days kept just busy enough to put her out of his mind for a time. Just yesterday, he'd thought he'd seen her in the crowd. But when he looked again, she was gone, a figment of his imagination.

He'd thought about calling her mother to find out if she'd returned home. But it wasn't fair to get her family involved in their fractured relationship.

When he reached the marina, Cameron pulled into his parking space. Since he'd returned to Seattle, he'd settled back into all of his old routines—Seahawks games on Sundays, Mariners games during the week, and on Friday afternoons he always went out sailing. It gave him time to clear his head, to reorganize his priorities—and to think about Sofie.

He always grabbed a latte from the shop across the street, the caffeine giving him a boost of energy after a long week of work. Looking both ways, Cameron jogged across the street to the Spinnaker, a favorite hangout for the local sailors.

He stepped to the counter and the barista smiled at him. "Sixteen-ounce triple-shot skim latte?" she asked.

"You got it," Cameron said.

"How does the weather look?" she asked. "I heard it was going to rain this afternoon."

Cameron chuckled. "Really. Doesn't it rain every afternoon? If I stayed in when it rained, I'd have to dust the cobwebs off my boat."

"No, the rain would wash them away," she teased.

He tossed four dollars on the counter and took the latte from her, then turned for the door. Just as he was ready to walk out, a voice stopped him.

"Cameron?"

He held his breath as he slowly turned around. And when he saw her, standing in the middle of the coffee shop, he let it out. She looked more beautiful than he remembered, and he reached out and grabbed her hand, just to make sure she was real. "Sofie," he murmured.

"Hi," she said, giving his hand a squeeze.

He wasn't sure what to say. He had so many questions, but none of them seemed to matter right now. "This is the last place I expected to see you."

"I knew I'd find you here," she said. "You come here every Friday before you go sailing."

"How do you know that?"

"I'm a trained detective. I know all kinds of things."

Cameron shook his head. "Where have you been?"

"Here," Sofie said.

"In Seattle?"

She nodded. "Yeah. I came up after I left New Mexico. I—I wanted to check the place out. To see if it was a good fit. I've got a temporary job with the Seattle Police Department as a dispatcher. I work mostly on the weekends and some evenings."

"Wait a minute. You've been here the whole time? Even when I wasn't?"

"Can we sit?" she asked, glancing around. "I feel kind of conspicuous standing here."

"Come on. We'll go to my boat. It's just across

the street in the—" Cameron paused. "I expect you know exactly where it is."

"It's a really nice boat," she said with a hesitant smile.

He took her hand as they crossed the street, the simple gesture a confirmation that his feelings hadn't faded. Just touching her was enough to set his pulse racing. He could barely take his eyes off her.

Cameron stopped at his car and retrieved his bag from the trunk, then slung it over his shoulder. He held the gate open as she walked through the gate, then followed her down the pier.

"Callisto," she said, staring at the name painted on the stern. "One of the moons of Jupiter. It's a pretty name."

"I thought of the name before I built the boat," he said.

"You built this?"

"I designed it. And I built a lot of it, but I had help. It's hull number three for me. The third hull I designed. One of my favorites."

He tossed his bag into the cockpit, then stepped from the pier onto the deck. Cameron held out his hand.

"Aren't I supposed to ask you if I can come aboard?"

"No. You're always welcome."

She hopped across the gap to stand beside him, wavering slightly as she regained her balance. "I've never been on a boat this big before. I've been on fishing boats, but that's it."

"Would you like a tour?" he asked, drawing her down into the cockpit. Cameron set his coffee down in the rack near the wheel, then turned back to her.

"Not really," she said.

"Something to eat?"

"I'm not hungry." Sofie drew a sharp breath.

"You know, I thought I saw you. Yesterday, I was at Pike Place, and I thought I caught a glimpse of you in the crowd and—"

"You did," she said. "I followed you there. I was going to talk to you, but then I chickened out. I came today instead." Sofie took a ragged breath. "I—I really think it might be best if you kiss me. I mean, just to get it out of the way. So things aren't so awkward."

Cameron wrapped his arm around her waist and drew her closer. "I think I can manage that."

As his mouth met hers, Cameron was stunned at the intensity of his feelings. He'd worked so hard not to miss her that he hadn't even realized how deep the void had been. And now she was here, filling him up again until it seemed as if they'd just seen each other yesterday.

When he finally drew back, he looked down into her beautiful face and saw tears glittering in her eyes. "Don't cry," he whispered. "This isn't supposed to be sad. We're supposed to be happy."

"I can't help it. I've been thinking about this moment for six weeks."

"Six weeks and three days," he said.

"Yes. Six weeks and three days. And even though I've imagined this moment a million times, it was so much better than I'd hoped."

"I could try to make it even better, if you'd like," Cameron said, wagging his eyebrows. He kissed her again, this time wrapping his arms around her waist and picking her up, their bodies molding to each other.

"We still fit," she said.

"Lucky thing," he said. "Nothing has changed, Sofie. I'm still in love with you. And I'm willing to do whatever it takes to make it work. You just say the word."

"What is the word?"

"Yes?"

"What am I agreeing to?" she asked.

"A lifetime of happiness. A man who'll do everything in his power to protect you and to treasure you. A future filled with laughter and love. Anything you want, Sofie, I'll make it yours."

She stared up into his eyes for a long moment, and Cameron thought she might refuse his offer yet again. But then she nodded. "I'd like that. I'd like to make a life with you, Cameron. And I'm thinking we should stay in Seattle. I'd like to learn how to sail."

"You really want to live in Seattle?"

"It rains here. Almost every day. Do you know how wonderful that is? I've learned to enjoy long walks in the rain."

"And what else do you like about Seattle?"

"I can get a fabulous cup of coffee on every street corner."

"And?"

She laughed. "And you're here. Since you're my guy, this is exactly where I need to be."

Cameron dragged her into another kiss, then pulled her onto the cushioned seats in the cockpit. "God, I've missed you. Don't ever do this to me again."

"I promise, I won't."

He pressed a kiss to her neck and then sat up. "So, do you think we should sail this boat or should I show you the bed?"

"There's a bed?" Sofie asked.

Cameron nodded. "A big, comfortable bed, just belowdecks."

"I think I'd like to try that out."

He grabbed her waist and pulled her to her feet. He'd never had a woman on his boat before and wanted to christen it right. "Welcome to our future, Sofie Reyes," Cameron said.

"It's going to be a beautiful future," she said. "Just like in my dreams."

Epilogue

TALIE REYES PICKED UP the stack of letters that the mailman had left on the rear counter of the gallery. Her attention was caught by two large boxes sitting on the floor, but she flipped through the envelopes anyway.

When she came across one with Sofie's handwriting on the envelope, she smiled. Though she and Sofie spoke weekly via Skype, they also carried on correspondence by mail. The letters, unlike their conversations over the computer, were filled with all of Sofie's dreams for her future, all of the things she wished for.

Talie opened the envelope and pulled out a page torn from a wedding magazine. *"Dear Mama,"* she read. *"Well, it happened. I was so nervous and so was he, but Cameron wasn't going to let anything— or anyone—stop him. We were taking a sail, and just as the sun touched the horizon, he got down on one knee and asked if I'd marry him. Of course, I said yes. I didn't have a moment's hesitation. I knew it was exactly what I wanted. Oh, Mama, you were so right. He makes me laugh and he makes me feel beautiful and I trust him completely. I just needed to be patient and it all became clear. We're planning a summer wedding in Albuquerque, and I'm going to need your help because I have no idea what I'm doing. Please don't tell Papa yet. Cameron wanted to ask his permission first, so he hadn't even bought a ring yet.*

"I have to go! I'll write more later. Love you! Sofie. Oh, the picture is a wedding dress I like. When I come home we have to go shopping for a gown. I refuse to set foot in a shop without you."

Talie smiled to herself as she slipped the letter back into the envelope. She'd always known the time would come when her daughter would need her advice. It was sad that she was so far away, but she couldn't feel too bad. Her daughter had found a new dream for herself—a man, a home and maybe soon, a family.

"Take a breath of the new dawn," she murmured to herself, "and make it part of you."

* * * * *

COMING NEXT MONTH from Harlequin® Blaze™
AVAILABLE OCTOBER 16, 2012

#717 THE PROFESSIONAL
Men Out of Uniform
Rhonda Nelson
Jeb Anderson might look like an angel, but he's a smooth-tongued devil with a body built for sin. Lucky for massage therapist Sophie O'Brien, she knows just what to do with a body like that....

#718 DISTINGUISHED SERVICE
Uniformly Hot!
Tori Carrington
It's impossible to live in a military town without knowing there are few things sexier than a man in uniform. Geneva Davis believes herself immune...until hotter than hot Marine Mace Harrison proves that a military man *out* of uniform is downright irresistible.

#719 THE MIGHTY QUINNS: RONAN
The Mighty Quinns
Kate Hoffmann
When Ronan Quinn arrives in Sibleyville, Maine, he finds not just a job, but an old curse, a determined matchmaker and a beautiful woman named Charlie. But is earth-shattering sex enough to convince him to give up the life he's built in Seattle?

#720 YOURS FOR THE NIGHT
The Berringers
Samantha Hunter
P.I. in training Tiffany Walker falls head-over-heels in lust for her mentor, sexy Garrett Berringer. But has she really found the perfect job *and* the perfect man?

#721 A KISS IN THE DARK
The Wrong Bed
Karen Foley
Undercover agent Cole MacKinnon hasn't time for a hookup until he rescues delectable Lacey Delaney after her car breaks down. But how can he risk his mission—even to keep the best sex of his life?

#722 WINNING MOVES
Stepping Up
Lisa Renee Jones
Jason Alright and Kat Moore were young and in love once, but their careers tore them apart. Now, fate has thrown them together again and given them one last chance at forever. But can they take it?

You can find more information on upcoming Harlequin® titles, free excerpts and more at www.Harlequin.com.

REQUEST YOUR FREE BOOKS!
2 FREE NOVELS PLUS 2 FREE GIFTS!

❧ Harlequin®
Blaze™

red-hot reads!

YES! Please send me 2 FREE Harlequin® Blaze™ novels and my 2 FREE gifts (gifts are worth about $10). After receiving them, if I don't wish to receive any more books, I can return the shipping statement marked "cancel." If I don't cancel, I will receive 6 brand-new novels every month and be billed just $4.49 per book in the U.S. or $4.96 per book in Canada. That's a saving of at least 14% off the cover price. It's quite a bargain. Shipping and handling is just 50¢ per book in the U.S. and 75¢ per book in Canada.* I understand that accepting the 2 free books and gifts places me under no obligation to buy anything. I can always return a shipment and cancel at any time. Even if I never buy another book, the two free books and gifts are mine to keep forever.

151/351 HDN FEQE

Name   (PLEASE PRINT)

Address   Apt. #

City   State/Prov.   Zip/Postal Code

Signature (if under 18, a parent or guardian must sign)

Mail to the **Reader Service:**
IN U.S.A.: P.O. Box 1867, Buffalo, NY 14240-1867
IN CANADA: P.O. Box 609, Fort Erie, Ontario L2A 5X3

Not valid for current subscribers to Harlequin Blaze books.

Want to try two free books from another line?
Call 1-800-873-8635 or visit www.ReaderService.com.

* Terms and prices subject to change without notice. Prices do not include applicable taxes. Sales tax applicable in N.Y. Canadian residents will be charged applicable taxes. Offer not valid in Quebec. This offer is limited to one order per household. All orders subject to credit approval. Credit or debit balances in a customer's account(s) may be offset by any other outstanding balance owed by or to the customer. Please allow 4 to 6 weeks for delivery. Offer available while quantities last.

Your Privacy—The Reader Service is committed to protecting your privacy. Our Privacy Policy is available online at www.ReaderService.com or upon request from the Reader Service.

We make a portion of our mailing list available to reputable third parties that offer products we believe may interest you. If you prefer that we not exchange your name with third parties, or if you wish to clarify or modify your communication preferences, please visit us at www.ReaderService.com/consumerschoice or write to us at Reader Service Preference Service, P.O. Box 9062, Buffalo, NY 14269. Include your complete name and address.

*Bestselling Harlequin® Blaze™ author Rhonda Nelson
is back with yet another irresistible Man out of Uniform.
Meet Jebb Willington—former ranger, current security
agent and all-around good guy. His assignment—to catch
a thief at an upscale retirement residence. The problem—
he's falling for sexy massage therapist Sophie O'Brien,
the woman he's trying to put behind bars....*

Read on for a sneak peek at
THE PROFESSIONAL

Available November 2012 only from Harlequin Blaze.

Oh, hell.

Former ranger Jeb Willingham didn't need extensive army training to recognize the telltale sound that emerged roughly ten feet behind him. He was Southern, after all, and any born-and-bred Georgia boy worth his salt would recognize the distinct metallic click of a 12-gauge shotgun. And given the decided assuredness of the action, he knew whoever had him in their sights was familiar with the gun and, more important, knew how to use it.

"On your feet, hands where I can see them," she ordered.

He had to hand it to her. Sophie O'Brien was cool as a cucumber. Her voice was steady, not betraying the slightest bit of fear. Which, irrationally, irritated him. He was a strange man trespassing on her property—she ought to be afraid, dammit. Why hadn't she stayed in the house and called 911 like a normal woman?

Oh, right, he thought sarcastically. Because she wasn't a *normal* woman. She was kind and confident, fiendishly clever and sexy as hell.

He wanted her.

And the hell of it? Aside from the conflict of interest and the tiny matter of *her name at the top of his suspect list?*

She didn't like him.

"Move," she said again, her voice firmer. "I'd rather not shoot you, but I will if you don't stand up and turn around."

Beautiful, Jeb thought, feeling extraordinarily stupid. He'd been an army ranger, one of the fiercest soldiers among Uncle Sam's finest…and he'd been bested by a massage therapist with an Annie Oakley complex.

With a sigh, he got up and flashed a grin at her. "Evening, Sophie. Your shrubs need mulching."

She gasped, betraying the first bit of surprise. It was ridiculous how much that pleased him. "You?" she breathed. "What the hell are you doing out here?"

He pasted a reassuring look on his face and gestured to the gun still aimed at his chest. "Would you mind lowering your weapon? It's a bit unnerving."

She brought the barrel down until it was aimed directly at his groin. "There," she said, a smirk in her voice. "Feel better?"

Has Jebb finally met his match? Find out in
THE PROFESSIONAL

Available November 2012
wherever Harlequin Blaze books are sold.

HARLEQUIN *Presents*®

Find yourself
BANISHED TO THE HAREM
in a glamorous and tantalizing new tale from

Carol Marinelli

Playboy Sheikh Prince Rakhal Alzirz has time for
one more fling in London before he must return
to his desert kingdom—and Natasha Winters has
caught his eye. He seizes the chance to discover if
Natasha is as fiery in bed as her flaming red hair,
but their recklessness has consequences…. She
might be carrying the Alzirz heir!

BANISHED
TO THE HAREM

Available October 16!

www.Harlequin.com

HP13103